ST. MARY PARISH LIBRARY

3 3446 00804 5896

CAC   Cachet.
          Make sure she knows
          about me   PAT

Make Sure She Knows About Me

Written by:

Cachet

&

Angie Hayes

D1528413

ST. MARY PARISH LIBRARY
FRANKLIN, LOUISIANA

Make Sure She Knows About Me

©Copyright 2017 Cachet & Angie Hayes

Published by:
Diamond Divas Publications

All rights reserved. No part of this book may be used or reproduced in any manner whatsoever without written permission from the publisher, except where permitted by law.

This is a work of fiction. Any resemblance to actual persons living or dead is purely coincidental.

First Trade Paperback Edition Printing 2017

ISBN-13: 978-1548103040
ISBN-10: 1548103047

Dedication

(Cachet)

This book is dedicated to my husband, Stephen Andres Sr., and my children; Keiasya, Tre'Maine, Stephen Jr., Zaria. You guys are the greatest.

More books by Cachet

When He Cheatin' And You Still Love Him 1 & 2
This Could Be Us But You Playin' 1-3
A Savage In Heels 1 & 2
Unstable Union
Shawty Got A Thang For Bad Boys And Fame

Stay in Touch

Email: AuthorCachet@gmail.com
Facebook: Facebook.com/AuthoressCachet
Author Page: AuthorCachet
Instagram: __Cachet__
Twitter: CachetNicole

Dedication

(Angie)

To Shavargo, my human Teddy; I love you more than words can express. Thank you for being my forever

More books by Angie Hayes

From Mistress To Wife 1-3
Yo' Boo Been Creepin' With Me 1-3
His Love Vs Her Lust
Even The Preacher Got A Side Chick 1-3
It Was Always Us: Love In These Miami Streets 1-3

Stay in Touch

Email: Mrshayes33147@hotmail.Com
Facebook: Facebook.com/Angie Hayes
Author Page: Angie Hayes
Instagram: hayesworld_4eva
Twitter: Armywife33147

INTRODUCTION

"So, you think you can just come in this muthafucka and tell me that you're all of a sudden going out of town and I'm supposed to be cool with that shit? Nigga you must be out your damn mind! I already know that you're going to go be with that bitch!" I yelled jumping up in Ethan face.

"I don't have time for this shit Chace, I told you that it was a last-minute meeting that I have to attend" Ethan said as he was packing his bag.

"Last minute meeting my ass! Do I look like I'm a damn fool to you? You must forget that I'm the bitch that has been with you since the beginning of time, and the one you married! I'm the one that knows you Ethan. From the way your tape line is supposed to be when you get a haircut, to when it's time for your ass to clip your fucking toe nails! Stop trying to play me like these simple-minded chicks you deal with out here Ethan!"

"There you go with this shit again. I don't have time to

pacify your ass, neither do I have time to convince you that this is only a business meeting that I'm going to alone. You can take this shit how you want, but I'm gone. I'll holla at you when I touch down in Dallas." Ethan left out the room with his duffle bag in tow.

Minutes later, I heard the front door down stairs slam shut. Muthafucka ain't even ask me to take his ass to the airport, that's how I know he's taking another hoe with him on this last-minute trip he suddenly had to take. I know you all are wondering, *what's going on and who are these people?* Well, my name is Chase McKenzie, and the bastard you just heard me go off on, was my husband, Ethan McKenzie. Now the *hoe* who you heard me referring to, that was probably going on this business trip with him, is just some other free pussy he fucking this month.

If you know he's cheating, then why are you still with him? Others number one question others love to ask in situations like this. Well, once you come into my world and hear my story, you'll understand why I'm not giving up on staying Mrs. McKenzie....

CHAPTER 1

Chace

My name is Chace McKenzie, and it has been for the last five years. I've been with my husband, Ethan for a total of ten years though. We met our sophomore year of high school in the hard knock streets of Chicago. I was born and raised there to a momma who was on dope, did anything and anyone to feed her habit, and lawd knows who the fuck my daddy is. Shit, he probably was the damn ice cream man for all I know. Anyways, I was the youngest, and the only girl with two older brothers. My brothers did their best to try and fill in the *daddy* role for me, but deep down, I always longed for my real father, so that I could know what it felt like to actually have one in my life.

When I was fifteen, some young ass, corner boy, killed my mother after she tried to snatch his dope from his hand, when he was trying to make a sale. He chased her down and shot her right in the back of the head in a nearby alley. Around that time, my oldest brother, Marquise, was eighteen and had already dropped out of school; and was also slanging on the corner. My other brother, Markell, who was sixteen in high school with me, somehow managed to be the total opposite, and the star on the basketball team for our school.

When we got the news about our mother, Markell seemed to be the only one affected by her murder; as to where Marquise and I, just felt relief. It was no secret how bad her habit was, so Marquise and I knew that it was only a matter of time before it would cost her to lose her life. Besides, around the time of her murder, my mother hadn't been home for three month's prior; which resulted to my brothers and I pretty much taking care of ourselves.

Marquise took on the roll, as the man of the house, and made sure that Markell and I stayed in school. He also made it clear that he would be the one providing for us, and that's exactly what he did. It was the first day of school, the beginning of my sophomore year, and already, I was ready for this shit to end. I didn't hang around other bitches at the school like that, because they always seemed to have some type of beef and be on some jealous shit.

Being raised by my brother, made my hands lethal. So, after I had to beat a couple of bitch's asses for trying me, they knew to keep my name out of their mouth, and keep it moving! As far as the dudes go, they were too scared to approach me, because of who my brothers were; so, they stayed out of my way as well. I had just gotten my schedule, and was standing at my locker looking it over, when I noticed this new face coming my way.

This guy stood out a lot. Not only was he tall, but he was fine as fuck! He stopped at a locker, three locks down from mines, and put some books in there. When he was done, he closed it, and looked right at me smiling; displaying his perfect teeth. I immediately blushed, but looked away. This was the first time a dude had ever made me blush, and I liked that shit.

Out the corner of my eyes, I saw some other hoes whispering and trying to check dude out as well. Since he was fresh meat, I knew right then and there that I had to snatch his ass up quick. That dude ended up being my husband today, Ethan McKenzie. Ethan and I had been rocking hard for the rest of our high school years. Hoes knew that when they saw him, that was all me, and that's how I wanted it. Bitches knew not to try me about my man. Ethan and I grew up differently. He moved to Chicago to live with his grandmother after his mom and dad were killed in a plane crash. Ethan was the only child, and his grandmother was all he had, until I came along of course.

Never the less, we were known around school as being together, and even voted as best couple in the yearbook. Ethan was smart when it came to his books, where as to I did just enough to get by. Ethan always stayed on his shit, and tried to keep me on mines. When we got to our senior year, it was then, that he really started trying to buckle down on me about getting serious on my studies. He had plans on going to college, and wanted me to be right by his side, but I wasn't feeling that.

I mean, I wanted to be with my man and all, but I just didn't see college in my future. Hell, I couldn't wait to graduate from fucking high school. Besides, Marquise had moved up in the dope game, and was now running his own little operation. Markell ended up busting his knee in a championship game, which blew his chances of his basketball scholarship; So, he was now heavy in the game with my brother making major dough.

I never mentioned to Ethan that I didn't want to go to college. So, every time he would bring it up, I would just change the subject instead. All throughout our senior year, he was receiving offer letters from schools all over. I was afraid that Ethan was going to go to a school out of state, and forget about me. I was far from being a dummy, to think that a nigga was going be faithful while being in a long-distance relationship. Hell, I didn't even know if I would be faithful my damn self. I was smart enough to know that shit happens, and people have needs; especially dudes.

It was prom night when Ethan announced to me, that he chose to stay in Chicago for college, and go to Northeastern

Illinois University, so that he could be closer to me and his grandma. I was so damn happy, that I gave my man some ass that night. I know that shit is cliché with fucking on prom night, but after making him wait for two years to get this pussy, that was the perfect time to bust it open for his fine ass.

That night, was the first-time Ethan and I had sex, or me having sex ever. So, not only did Ethan break my virginity, but I also ended up getting pregnant the first time. My brothers weren't all that pissed when I told them about my pregnancy, because they knew Ethan was a good dude. Ethan was even excited, but I wasn't.

I love him, but I definitely didn't want to be tied down with no fucking baby. So, what did I do? The day after graduation, I went and secretly got an abortion. Shit, I just couldn't see myself being somebody momma, especially when mines was so fucked up before she was killed. I caught the bus to the clinic earlier that day, and caught a cab back home that day when the procedure was done; with Ethan thinking I was out job hunting.

When I got home that afternoon, I laid down and tried to sleep the pain away. Shortly after falling asleep, I woke up in my bed, with blood between my legs, and had to be rushed to the hospital. I was in so much pain, but it actually worked in my favor having to go to the hospital. I had the doctor tell my brothers and Ethan, that I had miscarried, instead of just having had an abortion; you know, the whole doctor, patient confidentially shit.

After that ordeal, I had to play the role as a *grieving woman*, who was so sad that she had just lost her baby. I convinced Ethan that it was too emotionally draining, to think about having another child, and that I was also too scared to go through that type lost again. I got on birth control after that, and had been taking that muthafucka faithfully.

Right when it was time for Ethan to go away to college, his grandmother became ill with cancer. It was tearing him up to see her suffer like that, and me as well. His grandmother was always nice to me, and treated me as if I was her granddaughter. Ethan had to postpone him going to college in the fall like he had originally planned, which caused him to lose his scholarship.

I started seeing my man fall apart after that, and it was eating me up. At the time, I wasn't doing shit but looking fly, and being on every scene. So, when the opportunity came, I asked my brothers to give me a position in their organization. I wasn't trying to be one of those bitches that bagged up the dope with their titties hanging out and shit like you see in the movies, Nah, I wanted a position where I didn't have to get my hands dirty and still get paid.

I already knew they weren't going to put me in harm's way, so I became the head bitch in charge over collecting the money. My job was to make sure that all the trap houses numbers were on point, and that money I collected was counted for. If so much as a dollar bill was missing, their momma would be sitting the front pew, crying over their ass laid in the casket. Although I was on their payroll, my brothers still took care of me, and made sure I wanted for nothing. So, what did I do with the money I got from being on my brother's payroll? I used every bit of it to send my nigga to college!

You never heard that shit before huh? A female who is in the drug game, sending her man to college. Usually, it's the other way around, but I was that type of bitch. I figured, since Ethan was smart and taking up business management, that when he graduated, we both could run a fucking Empire together and make this money the right way. His job was to go to school, get those grades, and not fuck other bitches, and the rest would be taken care of; and that's exactly what he did.

Everything worked out fine, that we ended up getting married soon as Ethan graduated from college, and I became pregnant with our daughter Imani. Ethan ended up getting a job at a sports agency firm where he interned at, but I told him that I wanted him to be his own boss instead. So, I gave him the startup money to start his own firm: McKenzie Management.

My husband started out with two clients, who happened to graduate from the same college as him, and became professional baseball players. We all know baseball players are one of the highest paid athletes. Ethan worked hard to make sure that his two clients stayed that way. Now, here it is, years later, and he has over one hundred clients that his firm represents, and about two hundred employees under his belt. McKenzie Management is known worldwide in the sports world. We ended up settling in New York, because it was one of the biggest states known, as to where all the athletes, sports entertainers, rapper, and so on lived. Ethan and I have more money coming in that we could ever need, and I live a life bitches could dream of. If you haven't figured it out by now, it was me who made all this possible. Now, you have a better understanding why I'm not so easy into giving up my husband to the next hoe, who decides that she can suck his dick better than I can. I molded Ethan, and I'd be damn if another bitch reaps these benefits.

CHAPTER 2

Kennedi

"You know what, Mook? I really don't have time for this," I sighed as I placed another pair of stilettos inside my suitcase. "I have to leave out to catch my flight in a few, and I have to be ready when the driver gets here."

"Well, I need to talk to you, so you better make time," he urged, "That damn plane ain't going nowhere!" I could hear the irritation in his voice and didn't care one damn bit. "You've been ducking and dodging me for weeks, and before I get off this muthafuckin' phone you gone have to tell me something."

"First of all, I don't have to tell you shit!" I shot back angrily. "You got caught up once again and there is nothing else left for us to talk about. I don't know how many times I have to say the same fucking thing over and over again because clearly, yo' ass ain't listening. It's over!"

"Come on now, Pook—"

"My name is Kennedi," I cut him off preventing him from speaking the nickname that only my best friend is allowed to call me. It's usually Pookie, but she sometimes shortens it to Pook at times.

"Damn, so it's like that, huh?" he asked, but when I didn't

reply he continued. "Anyway, you know damn well that girl was lying about everything she told you," he rationalized, "All that bullshit she was hollin' was nothing but lies. On top of that, how you gone believe a bitch that you already know don't like you in the first place? You know she ain't doing shit but trying to piss you off, and you letting her."

As he continued to lie, all I could do was shake my head, because he really thought I was a fool. Well, I guess I had been for years when it came to him. A fool for believing all of the lies he told. I can't even pretend like I didn't know better, because I did. Unfortunately for him, things have changed and I'm no longer the naive chick that he's used to dealing with.

"Dude, the only reason she doesn't like me is because of yo' ass. That damn girl doesn't even know me for real, so how in the hell can she not like me?" I asked, but of course, he doesn't say anything right away. Taking his silence as an urge for me to continue, I keep going on, letting him know that he has a lot of nerve. "The fact that you chose to fuck with a bitch who you claim I should already know doesn't like me, is even more of a slap in the face, with yo' disrespectful ass! Then you're sitting on this phone talking shit about her when she was yo' boo thang not too long ago. So, please stop the madness, withcho lying ass," I scoff.

"Bullshit! I keep telling you that I wasn't fucking with that girl! How many times do I have to keep saying it?"

"You can say it until you're blue in the damn face, and I still won't believe you or give a fuck!" I snapped. "You're a liar, Mook, and I'm tired of playing games with you."

"Stop trying to play me, man. I wasn't fucking with the hoe, and I ain't lying."

Heading into my bathroom, I grabbed my toiletries bag and flat irons off the counter before making my way back into my bedroom. "Now she a hoe," I laughed. "Alright, I guess I'm deaf, blind and stupid, huh?"

He sighed. "See, I ain't say that. Now you putting words in my mouth."

"No, I'm just calling it how I see it," I paused. "You know what?

I don't even know why I keep entertaining you and your lies. " I waved my hand dismissively as if he could see actually see me. "You must have forgotten that I busted you and her coming out of the movie theater not too long ago." My voice was calm as I placed my things into my suitcase.

"I told you I wasn't there with her! I went by my damn self," he lied. "It ain't my fault that she just happened to be there too."

"Yeah, okay. You can say what you want, and make up every excuse in the world, but the fact still remains that I'm tired," I told him honestly. "I don't want to do this anymore, Mook. You can have all those hoes you be dealing with. You ain't gotta worry about me popping up on you no more. I'm tired of going through your phone and driving myself crazy wondering what you're out here doing while I'm not around. You're free now, so do you, boo. All I'm asking is that you just leave me the fuck alone." Just saying those words aloud made my heart hurt a little bit. Even though I was in fact, tired of all the things that he'd put me through, he was all I've ever known, and it upset me to know that things had come to this.

Darnell 'Mook' Ware and I have been dating for the last five years. He was my first boyfriend, first sex partner and first true love. We met through my best friend, Tasha, when I was seventeen after her mother married his father, Darnell Sr. I remember the first time I saw Darnell. He was so damn fine! It was the day they were moving in the house that Tasha shared with her mother. I was coming out of the bathroom, and Darnell had just made it to the top of the stairs with a large box in his hands. As he passed by me a few of the CD's that were stacked on top of his things fell, so I bent down to grab them for him. As I stood back up with them in my hand, my shoulder hit the bottom of the box, and before Darnell had a chance to react, the entire thing went flying out of his hands. As it fell, even more of his stuff spilled out and landed all over the carpeted floor. To say that I was mortified was an understatement. To make matters worse, once I attempted to help him clean up the mess I'd made, I hurt myself. While grabbing a bunch of stuff at once, I ended up slicing my hand open with an opened box cutter. I damn near passed out it was so much blood.

That night I wound up in the emergency room with ten stitches across my palm. Darnell apologized over and over again, because he felt bad for what had happened, even though I let him know that it wasn't his fault. I, on the other hand, was more worried about the fact that I had embarrassed myself more than I was about my hand actually being cut. After that crazy day, since Darnell now lived in the same house as my best friend, I saw him all of the time. With him being three years older than Tasha and I, he had much more free reign than we did. Since he and his dad had relocated from Mississippi to Georgia, Darnell didn't know anyone other than the people in their household, so he pretty much kicked it with Tasha and I a lot.

The fact that he was Tasha's step-brother sat well with my parents, and because of that, we were allowed kick it with him all around the city; especially after Darnell promised to always keep an eye on us. It's crazy, but not too crazy, because everyone assumed that because he was now related to Tasha, that I looked at him as a brother as well. They couldn't have been more wrong. I was crushing on him something terrible and looked forward to seeing him every weekend. Darnell was like a new drug, and I couldn't wait to test the high.

I was a few months' shy of my eighteenth birthday when I found out that I wasn't alone with my feelings. Tasha and I were having our usual weekend sleepover. That night it was at her house. We were in the living room watching a movie, and like always she was knocked out before the movie really got going. Since I was used to her falling to sleep, I continued to watch the film, while munching on the popcorn that we'd made. Right before the credits rolled Darnell strolled in. He had just finished his shift at his job and was looking for something to eat since Tasha's mother hadn't cooked anything. Although I'd had eaten pizza earlier with Tasha, I was hungry again, so when he asked if I wanted to run with him to McDonald's to grab some burgers, I was down. After getting us both value meals, neither of us wanted to go back to the quiet house, so we rode around just listening to music. It felt so good to be not only out but to be alone with Darnell. As we rode around, I pictured that he was my boyfriend, and I was his girl. Looking back, it was stupid, but I swear back then you couldn't keep the smile off of my face. I was cheesing and shit like I'd hit the lotto.

Anyway, before long Darnell started to ask me questions. At first, he started out with little things like what I planned to do for my birthday, and if I planned on going to college after graduation. Once I answered those questions, he got a little more person. He then wanted to know why I didn't have a boyfriend. My slow ass didn't catch on at first because I really thought that he looked at me like I was just another little sister, and I thought he was doing the average big brother thing by trying to see where my head was at when it came to dude. Those thoughts went out of the window when we pulled into Tasha's driveway and Darnell leaned over and kissed me on the lips. I was so shocked I didn't know what to do because all that time I thought he looked at me like a little sister. That moment was kind of surreal because even at almost eighteen, I had never dealt with a guy on that level. I mean, I talked on the phone to boys, but

17

nothing much more than that. Doing well in school was pretty much my main focus, and other than spending time with Tasha, I didn't have much time for anything else. I guess I was what you would call a good girl, which was apparently rare and one of the reasons why Darnell liked me so much.

That night in the car, he explained how he'd liked me for a while, and he didn't say anything because he didn't know exactly how to tell me. With our three-year age difference, Darnell didn't want anyone to think that he was a pervert, even though I was already seventeen. Shockingly, I spilled the beans as well. For some reason, I was no longer shy about being around him. After talking for more than an hour, we both agreed not to mention the fact that we were 'talking' until after my birthday. It killed me not to tell Tasha my secret, and before that week was out, I told her everything. She was happy for us and promised to keep our secret as well. Two months later, I turned eighteen and was officially a grown woman. Darnell waited a few days before he officially asked me to be his girl, and before long we became an actual couple; which turned out to not be a surprise to everyone around us who already knew that we liked one another.

Our relationship started out pretty good. We still did the same things when we got a chance to see each other, and he was still the same old Darnell. A few weeks later I graduated from school and walked across the stage with all of my loved ones in attendance. Even though I pretty much had my choice of colleges to go to, I decided to take a year or two off. I had no real reason to do that, and it was simply just due to the fact I was ready to take a break. During that time, I started to work at my father's realty company where I staged all of the homes that were up for sale. Since I had always loved to switch things around in our house, it was perfect for me, and the fact that I

had free reign to do what I pleased was a bonus.

It was then that things sped up between Darnell and I. He was no longer living in Tasha's house and his family and was living in an apartment on the other side of town. I practically lived there as well, because I was over there every single day; even more than I was at my own house. This went on for our entire first year together. I was so happy I didn't know what to do with myself.

By the time the New Year rolled around, I was working day in and day out. Not only had my father's company purchased more homes, but I was also picking up work from other companies as well. Due to me being so busy, I started to see Darnell less and less. It's no surprise that this put a strain on our relationship, but I figured that if we loved one another, we could work around my busy schedule. Baby, was I wrong! Soon he went from complaining about not seeing me as much, to not saying anything at all. Of course, I thought that it was because he understood that I had to work, but that wasn't the reason at all. It wasn't until a few months later that I found out that he hadn't been complaining because he was spending his time with another woman.

Finding out that Darnell was cheating, hurt me so bad. I couldn't believe that he would do something like that because he had always promised that he would never cause me pain. Yet, that's exactly what he'd done. I remember taking off work and staying in my room at my parent's house for the entire week crying. I barely ate anything and slept most of the day. Tasha came over and sat with me daily and each time she came, she asked if I wanted to jump Darnell's ass. Of course, I didn't, but that didn't stop her from rolling up on him one day. They had it out, with my best friend being the aggressor. Before it all said and done, Tasha threatened to cut his ass if he ever played me again.

My parents were both livid after they found out that he had broken my heart. After I literally had to beg my father not to go to Darnell's house and kick his ass, he and my mother sat me down and gave me a pep talk, before telling me to never allow him back into my life again. Their logic was, 'once a cheater, always a cheater,' and looking back, they were right. At that time, I agreed with them, because in my eyes, Darnell was a dog. Yeah, I talked a good game, but before long I allowed that dog and his dirty bone carrying ass to sweet-talk himself right back into my heart.

Darnell lied until he couldn't lie anymore. Seeing that I wasn't falling for the bullshit, he finally broke down and told me the truth; or at least his version of it. He said that it was a one-time thing, and claimed that it stemmed from me working so much and him feeling neglected. Just like a dummy, I believed him; even going as far as to feel bad for pretty much ignoring him. Looking back, I still don't know what the hell I was thinking to let his dog ass make me look at him as the victim but I did.

After taking Darnell back, things were cool; at least for a while. Now, five years later, I'm still going through the same exact bullshit and dealing with the constant lies. Every time I found out about another chick he was dealing with, I cried, and Darnell tried to get me back. It's been an ongoing cycle, but now I'm tired of it playing out the same way. It's like I'm stuck in a damn movie that keeps rewinding itself to the beginning and playing until the end. This time Darnell's broken promises are not going to work. I'm tired of hurting, sharing a man, and looking stupid as hell in the process. It's no secret that Darnell can't keep his penis in his pants. Everyone knows, they just don't say anything while I'm around. Instead, they choose to whisper the shit behind my back, and that in itself is a fucked up feeling to have.

"Look, I'm not about just let you go, so we're going to have to figure out something," Darnell told me as if I had no choice in the matter.

"Figure something out?" I sat the folded up blouse I was holding inside my suitcase and took a seat on the edge of my bed. "You have got to be kidding me, right?" I asked in disbelief. "Again, what part of, I'm tired and don't want to do this anymore, don't you fucking understand? I'm done, Mook, and there ain't shit that you can do about it," I told him.

"Oh, I heard you, and like I said I'm not letting you go."

A giggle slipped from my lips because I knew that he must have lost his damn mind. How in the hell can you tell someone that you're not going to let them go when you've cheated on them numerous times? Apparently, he wasn't thinking about not letting me go when he was straying like a fucking dog in heat. Even if he had been, this still isn't his call to make. Still amused by Darnell's behavior, I stood up and walked over to the window. When I saw the car that was going to take me to the airport had just pull into the parking lot, I quickly moved back over to my bed and tossed the last few items inside.

"I'm not about to go back and forth with you, Mook. I told you I'm done. You can say or think whatever the hell you want, but this here is over and there ain't shit you can do about it," I told him preparing to hang up my phone. He was really getting on my damn nerves.

"Yeah, okay… think I'm playing if you want to."

"Whatever!" I snapped. "I gotta go. I have a flight to catch."

"Cool. I'll see you when you touch back down."

Pulling my phone away from my ear, I looked at it with a
frown before I replied, "I doubt it."

"We'll see," he laughed.

"Boy bye!" I told him as Ii quickly zipped up my suitcase.

"Kennedi!" Darnell yelled just as I was about to hit the end button.

"What do you want, Mook?"

"I just wanted to let you know that I love you girl."

"Uh huh, that's nice. Bye."

This time I didn't give him a chance to say anything else to stop me. I had a plane to catch, and I'll be damn if I allowed his selfish ass to mess with my money. I'll deal with Darnell later. Right now I have to get downstairs to the car, so that I can make it to the airport on time for my flight. My destination is Miami, Florida, and I'm looking forward to having some fun in the sun. After I finish working my magic for my client, I'm going to let my hair down and relax. I'm young and newly single after all, and looking forward to having some fun.

CHAPTER 3

Chace

"Ooh, right there. That's right, lick all my juices." I moaned as I rotated my hips as his tongue was fucking my pussy.

I had already cum twice, and was on the verge of busting nut number three! Right when I was about to explode, my phone started ringing. By the ringtone, I already knew that it was Ethan. I quickly pushed dude head away from my box, and answered the phone.

"Hello." I answered trying to compose my breathing.

"Yeah, I need to head down to Miami for a last-minute business trip." Ethan immediately spoke, without even saying so much as a hello first.

"What do you mean you need to head to Miami?" I yelled into the phone sitting up.

"I just got word that Dwayne Wade just fired his Management Firm, and is looking our way to represent him. I wanna head out there personally, and make sure we reel him in." Ethan explained.

"OK cool, so I'll just meet you in Miami then." I suggested as I moved dude head again when he started licking on my inner thighs.

"I don't need any distractions right now Chace, so just stay home and I'll see you when I get there."

"Oh, so I'm a distraction now? You know all I'll be doing is shopping and doing my own thing." I fumed into the phone.

I knew Ethan was trying to throw excuses at me, as to why he didn't want me to come to Miami with him. I'm sure it was just so that he could fuck whomever he pleased without having to look over his shoulder.

"Look, I might have to entertain Dwayne Wade and his people, and show them a good time; and you know what that consist of. I don't have time to hear your nagging and bitching when you see other females around us, or in my ear when I'm coming back to the hotel late. I deal with that shit enough with you as it is." Ethan said sounding irritated.

The nerve of this bastard!

"Well, you wouldn't have to deal with my bullshit if you would find other ways to entertain these hoes instead of with your dick!" I shot back at his ass!

He had me fucked up if he thought that he was gonna make me out to be some type of jealous insecure bitch with no reasoning!

"Whatever Chace, I'll see you when I get home." Before I could respond, Ethan hung up the phone in my face.

I continued to lay there, with my phone still up to my ear, mad as hell. More and more, it seemed like Ethan was doing him, and slipping from me. It had become a routine now, with me catching him from time to time, with random hoes, whopping their asses, and trying to fuck him up as well in the process. Then, Ethan would come, kissing my ass and trying to make it up to me. His ass would buy me new diamonds, a car, fur, or whatever else it took to put just a little dent in his pockets. But now, Ethan has stepped his game up with taking these sudden trips out of town, and not letting me accompany him.

The thing about that is, Ethan does end up signing the new client he goes after. The money is steady pouring in, and the firm is rapidly growing. But, I'm not that naïve of a bitch, to think that his ass isn't also doing a little extra as well when he's away on those trips, and that extra, is dipping and dabbing in whichever bitch opens her legs or mouth.

"Damn baby, you just gone lay there with those sexy ass legs close, or you gone let a nigga finish feasting off that pussy." I heard Jerome say, breaking me from my thoughts.

I looked down at him, still waiting between my legs, with that sexy ass grin on his face. Ethan did just fuck up the mood calling with the bullshit, but, I needed to release this nut. I didn't respond to Jerome, Instead, I just opened my legs back wider, grabbed the back of his head, and guided him to my

honey pot.

The sensation of his tongue, cause me to arch my back, and squeeze on his shoulders.

"I'm about to cum baby." I moaned out loud.

Seconds later, I was releasing all my juices down Jerome throat, as he held down tight on my thighs and sucked me to the last drop. I was shaking, and breathing heavy as I tried to calm down from the orgasm I just had. Jerome got up, and went into the bathroom. I heard the water from the sink running. Minutes later, he came out of the bathroom, reached for his clothes off the back of the chair, and started putting them on.

"Why the hell are you getting dressed?" I asked confused, as I sat up on my elbows.

Normally, after Jerome ate my pussy, we get to straight fucking; and his ass has put me in the mood to do so.

"I need to go handle some business." Jerome replied as he continued to get dress.

"No, what you need to do is finish handling this business right here!" I opened my legs and started fingering my pussy.

"Yo ma, you need to chill out with all that demanding shit. I ain't your cornball ass husband, who you just got off the phone with. Besides, you lucky I let your ass get that last nut, since you wanna answer the phone and shit while we doing

us." Jerome said snidely shaking his head.

"Jerome, look, why don't you just take your clothes back off baby and get back in the bed. I promise, I'll make it worth your while." I licked my lips as I got up on my knees, and crawled to the edge of the bed where he was standing at getting dress.

"Nah, I'm good. I'll holla at you later; lock up when you leave" Jerome kissed me on my forehead, grabbed his keys off the night stand, and left.

Moments later, I heard his car music beating loud through the speakers as he cranked up, and pulled off. I reached over to the night stand, grabbed the blunt out the ash tray that we were smoking on earlier, and lit it. I laid back against the head board as I released the smoke from my mouth.

I knew once I answered the phone from Ethan, that Jerome would cop an attitude. But, shit, I was shocked that he was even calling, since I was the one doing the calling lately. I know what y'all are wondering, who the hell is

Jerome right? Well, Jerome is next in charge to my brothers in their business. That's right, he's a certified dope man, with the swag and dick game to match.

We had been fucking around for about two years now, and I must admit, his dick and tongue game has my ass hooked. All the niggas in brother circle wanted to fuck me, but they all knew that I was off limits to them. Jerome didn't give a damn what my brothers had to say, or that I had a husband, because he still approached me on the low, and it's been on ever since.

I figured, since Jerome had a hood rat ass baby momma, he was already dealing with, and I was married, that it would be strictly fucking between us. But lately, since Ethan has been flying his ass all over the states, I've been having more time to spend with Jerome. We've been meeting up frequently at his condo he has on the other side of town, fucking one another like crazy. Now, I know it seems like that I'm no better than Ethan, with fucking another nigga on the side; but, I didn't start messing around with Jerome until after Ethan fucked around on me.

I finished my blunt and went to take a quick shower. Once I was done, I got dress and headed out the door to go get my daughter, Imani from school. I had exactly forty minutes to make to her on time before school let out, or her grown ass would be telling her daddy that I was late picking her up again. I got in my Range, and drove off to hit the expressway.

CHAPTER 4

Kennedi

I just arrived in Miami, and I'm super excited. Although it's not my first time visiting the state, the last time work took longer than expected, and I wasn't able to much much before it time for me to head home. This time I plan to fully enjoy myself. While gripping my luggage, I make my way to the exit of the airport. As soon as I stepped out of the automatic doors, the heat caused my body temperature to immediately go up a few degrees. I'm thankful that I had decided to wear a cute, but thin summer dress and sandals instead of the jeans and t-shirt that I started to put on, or else I would have definitely been burning the hell up. With my roll-away luggage gripped tightly in my hand, I followed behind the Italian driver, who had recently introduced himself to me as Alfonso, over the all black town car, and waited as he opened the back door for me. Once I climbed inside, Alfonso closed the door and proceeded to take my luggage to the back of the car, where he placed it into the trunk. When he was finished, he climbed into the driver's seat.

"I've been instructed to take you to the Four Seasons, Ma'am. Is there anywhere you would like to go before then?" Alfonso asked glancing back at me through the rearview mirror.

"No, the hotel is fine," I replied removing my sunglasses from my eyes. "Will you be my driver during my entire stay, or will I have someone else?"

Alfonso smiled. "I'll be here to assist you for the remainder of your trip, Ma'am. Just let me know where you would like to go, and I'll be there to make sure you get there."

"Sounds good to me." I returned a smile of my own.

"Great. We'll be at the hotel in about twenty minutes."

"OK."

The soft black leather engulfed me as I leaned back and got comfortable for the ride. When Alfonso cranked up the car, it took a moment, but soon the air conditioning started to blow cool air through the vents. It felt so good against my warm skin that all I could do was close my eyes, moan and lay back against the headrest. When I felt us start to pull away from the curb, I opened my eyes and grinned. I really did love my job. The benefits of working with wealthy clientele are amazing, and whenever I'm on an assignment I'm always well taken care of. They made sure that I always had transportation to wherever I need to go, my hotel is paid for and all of my meals; on top of the payment I received for my services. It still amazes me just how far I've come over the last few years, and if someone would have told me that one picture would have changed my life so much, I would have thought that they were crazy.

A little over three years ago, my life drastically changed. I was still working for my father's company while picking up assignments from other businesses around town. Everything was going well for me, and I was making pretty good money. I had not only saved up enough to rent my own apartment but enough to furnish it as well. Around that time, Darnell and I were going back and forth arguing about his doggish way, and to be honest, I wanted my own space, so I went out and got just that. With my schedule still quite busy, I didn't have a lot of time to decorate my place, so I spruced up here and there during the week, as well as on the weekends when I was off. While I enjoyed making a room beautiful while I was on the job, to do it in my very own home was such a joy for me. I did it all. From painting accent walls in my bedroom to stenciling designs in the living room, I can honestly say that I worked hard. It took me all of three months to get my place exactly the way I wanted it to be.

Everything was perfect, and I was proud of myself for what I had created. The day I finished, I was walking around my apartment with a smile on my face when I decided to snap a few pictures. Soon after, I made a collage of the photos and sent it Tasha, who was then away at college. She was so pumped when she saw what I had done to the place that she went on to post the collage on Instagram to brag about her bestie's skills. Now, I had no clue that she had done that until I woke up the following morning with so many messages and tags on the social site that I couldn't keep up. Seeing my photos on there had me confused because it didn't register that I had sent them to my best friend, until a few minutes later. At first, I was kind of upset that Tasha had put pictures of the inside of my home on the site, but then I thought about the fact that people didn't actually know where I resided, I realized that it really wasn't really a big deal.

As the days went on, I continued to see my picture float around with the hashtag, #HomeGoals. It had been screenshotted and shared so many times, that it made its way to Facebook within the week. I was surprised to find out that I was a trending topic on both sites, as well as on Twitter. My inbox was blowing up. People were asking me for prices for my services, and at first, I ignored a lot of them. With so many scammers out here in this world, I figured they were just playing games. There was no way that someone would want to pay little old me to decorate their home, just off a few pictures that they've seen online. I mean, it was what I did as far as staging homes for selling purposes, but decorating homes for actual people didn't seem like something real. That was until I received a message from the wife of a point-guard for a team in Texas asking me if I would be available to do her home office. I'm not going to lie, at first I thought it was a joke, just like the others, and I'm not even sure why I responded to her message in the first place, but something in the back of my mind told me to. I started my message off by letting her know that I was leery about the situation, and she offered to call me to ease my fears.

That day we spoke on the phone, I found out that she was actually who she said she was. She explained that she and her husband had just recently purchased a new house, and she wanted her home office to be something comfortable, as well as cute. She said that she loved my pictures, and how I'd done the walls, and wanted me to do something similar to her place. When asked what my prices were, I was stuck and didn't really know what to say. Now I made decent money working for my father and the other companies that I dealt with, but talking to a wife of an NBA player was definitely a different league. Not wanting to mess things up, I asked her if I could call her back, and once she agreed I dialed up my father. Since he'd had his own company, and had been in business for well over twenty years, I knew that he would tell me exactly what I should do.

After chatting with my dad for close to an hour, I felt confident. I called the wife back and gave her price. Without even a pause in the conversation, she agreed to my fee, as well as the perks, and by the following week, I was on a plane to Dallas, on her dime. Once I arrived, it took me all of three days to transform her office, and when I was finished, the smile on her face let me know that I'd hit the nail on the head. Around that time the husband had shown up, and they both thanked me so much while letting me know that I was extremely talented and that they will definitely recommend me to their friends; which was music to my ears. I headed back home not only proud of myself, but with a hefty check in my purse as well. Of course, I tried to share half of it with Tasha, since she was the one who had made it all happen, but being the person she is, she declined before urging me to put her share back into my newly found business. While I agreed with what she'd said, that didn't stop me from depositing a large portion of the money into her account anyway. With her away in school, I knew that that money would come in handy when it came time to purchase books.

Immediately after I arrived back home, I began to get more messages, calls, and emails from all kinds of people.

From celebrities to regular folks who just wanted to change the way their homes looked. I'd be lying if I said that it didn't become a bit overwhelming because it did, but I rolled with the punches because like I said, I enjoyed what I did. I was traveling, and decorating for a few months when my father pulled me to the side and asked me what I planned to do with my newfound fame. At that time, I was just going with the flow and really didn't think about the future. When I told him that I was going to just do it for as long as I could, he gave me a jewel. My dad told me that if decorating was what I really wanted to do, then I should do it the right way and not half step.

After listening to his logic, I agreed with my father, and soon after I decided that it was time for me to stop procrastinating and go to college. It didn't take me long to choose a school with a good interior design program, and soon after I enrolled into The Savannah College of Art and Design. My next step was downtown, where I filled out all of my paperwork to start my own LLC, because I wanted to do things the correct way. With that part of my list of "to-do's" checked off, I hired a graphic designer that I found on Instagram, who created a logo and designed a website that displayed all of the photos that I had from the previous work that I'd done. With that all out of the way, Kennedi's

Kreations was in full effect. While I worked towards my degree, I continued to do jobs here and there. Well, that was three years ago, and now with an associate's degree in interior design, I'm one year away from my bachelors and couldn't be happier.

When I feel the car begin to slow up, I'm snapped out of my thoughts and see that we are now parked in front of the hotel. *That twenty minutes went fast*, I thought to myself as I sat up and glanced out of the window. Alfonso came around to my door and opened it. As I stepped out, he handed me the handle of my luggage, and as well as a card with his name and phone number on it. After I thanked him, I made my way into the hotel to check in. Since I didn't have to be at my client's house until tomorrow morning, I planned to chill out in the room for the remainder of the day. I had a full week to spend in Miami, and there was no rush. I planned to have my fun, but right now, I was going to take a nap.

*****

It took me four days to get everything together for the nursery for my client. She was a former Housewife of Atlanta cast member, who'd gotten pregnant with her fourth child. Her and her husband, an NFL player for the Atlanta

Falcons, had a home down in Miami and wanted to have a room for their new addition. Mrs. Kim, which is what I called her, was very meticulous and wanted everything to be perfect, so it took me awhile to get her on board with my ideas, and even needed the help of her two older daughters. Once I did though, everything went smooth from there. The end result was something straight out of a high fashion nursery magazine. Mrs. Kim couldn't thank me enough and showed her appreciation with a hefty bonus; which I gladly accepted.

With two days left in Miami, I decided to grab me something to eat, before I found something to get into. My work was done, and I was ready to finally let my hair down. Since I wasn't too familiar with the city, I decided to eat downstairs in the restaurant of the hotel. While sitting at the bar, I waited for the bartender to bring out my food. To pass the time I picked up my phone so that I can text Tasha and check on her since it had been few days since we'd spoke. When I did, I noticed that I had a few missed calls, and text messages from Darnell. Of course, I planned to ignore his ass just like I had been doing for the last few days. I already knew that once I arrived back in Savanna he was going to try his best to track me down, and I really wasn't looking forward to that at all.

Darnell had a way of being extremely persistent when he wanted to be, which is why we ended up staying together for as long as we did. He was the type of person who just wouldn't give up, no matter how many time I shot him down. At first, I used to think the shit was cute how hard he went to get me back, but now it's just annoying as fuck. All I want right now is for him to leave me the hell along and move the fuck on with his life because I definitely planned to.

"Let me get a Jack and Coke." I heard a baritone voice say. When I lifted my head, I locked eyes with a guy dressed in a seat who was standing only a few inches away with his hand on the barstool beside me. The tie and top button of his shirt are undone, and even with the more relaxed look he was rocking, he still gave off a professional vibe. He began to pull out the bar stool beside me when he abruptly stopped. "I'm sorry, but is this seat taken?" he asked when he noticed me staring at him.

"No, it's not. You're more than welcome to it," I replied looking back down at my phone. I started to type out the message that I was sending to Tasha. When I caught a whiff of the cologne that the guy wore, I glanced out of the corner of my eye and watched him take a seat.

"How's the food here?"

"It's pretty good." I nodded, "I've been eating here all week."

"Cool, I'm starved," he said while he rubbed his stomach for effect. I cut my eyes in his direction and giggled.

"What's funny?" he inquired as he grinned at me.

"Nothing." I continued to laugh, "It's just that when you walked up the first thing you asked for was a Jack and Coke. If you're so hungry, why didn't you order something to eat?"

"I don't know." He dropped his eyes. "I guess I just needed a drink."

Taking a sip of my margarita, I turned in his direction. It was then that I actually got a real good look at him, and I was pleased by what I saw. I smiled inwardly. He was a very handsome man that had a distinguished look about him. His chocolate skin tone was clear of any blemishes, and his goatee was trimmed without a hair out of place. A smooth bald head was what he rocked, and he had light brown eyes that complimented his dark skin tone and drew me in. If I had to guess, I would say that he was older than I was, but not by much, and only due to the fact that he was wearing a suit and tie. If he had been sporting a pair of jeans and a t-shirt, he would look much younger.

"Bad work week, huh?" I asked after I finished visually taking him in.

"That amongst other things," he sighed before he shook his head.

"Well, whatever it is, it can't be that bad. You're here alive and breathing."

"Yeah, you're right." When he smiled again, I got a good look at his teeth. They were perfectly straight and pearly white.
"You must be having a wonderful day."

I thought for a second, and instantly Darnell and his annoying ass ways came to mind. "Not really, but I won't complain."

"I need to be more like you."

"Don't say that," I laughed again. "My problems may just outweigh yours."

He smirked and gave me a side eye. "I seriously doubt that."

It hit me that I had been yapping with this man, and hadn't even introduced myself. Deciding to just contact Tasha later, I place my phone on the bar and stick my hand out in his direction.

"I'm sorry for being rude. I'm Kennedi, and you are?"

"You good. I'm the rude one. I was the one who walked up while you were sitting here, so it was me who should be apologizing," he told me flashing me yet another perfect smile. "Anyway, it's nice to meet you Kennedi. My name is, Ethan."

CHAPTER 5

Chace

It's been two weeks since Ethan had returned from his trip to Miami, and I'd be lying if I said that things were been back on track with us. Matter of fact, they seem to be getting worse. For starters, Ethan came home a week later than he was scheduled too, and since he's been back, his ass has been glued to that fucking phone like that shit was embedded into his hand! Then, the other night when I tried to wake his ass up with some head, he moved me from between his legs, rolled over, and started snoring.

The only person Ethan seems to be paying attention to at home was our daughter, and that was starting to irk my last nerves.

"Why don't we go out tonight to Club Price baby? My brothers are throwing a welcome home party for one of their boys who just did a bid." I suggested to Ethan, as I placed his plate of pancakes and turkey bacon in front of him.

I decided to get up this morning, and cook breakfast before he headed off to work. Priscilla, our housekeeper, takes Imani to school in the mornings; so she was already gone. It was Friday, and I knew Ethan would be getting off early, because he had a ritual of not working late on Fridays.

Besides, it had been a minute since we went out, and I felt like showing my husband off to these thirsty ass bitches, while shaking my ass in the process.

"I really don't feel like going to no club tonight, and celebrating one of your brother's jail bird ass friends, who will be right back in a cell a month later." Ethan snorted as he stuffed a bite of pancake into his mouth.

"Watch your damn mouth Ethan, because if it wasn't for those nigga's hustle, your ass wouldn't be sitting at this damn table acting like yo' shit don't stink!" I reminded him.

Ever since Ethan management company has prospered, and he didn't need my money any more to front him, Ethan started acting as if he was better than the muthafuckas out here hustling in the streets. I make sure to remind his ass every time he gets like this, that it was that same hustle of others, that got him where he is today. Plenty of times, my ass could have gotten locked up, making sure he never went without, and I damn sure didn't hear him complaining then.

"Oh boy, here we go with this shit again." Ethan yelled, out as he pushed his plate away from him.

"You damn right! Stop trying to look down on folks just because they make money different than you!"

"I make money the legal way Chace, so there is no comparison." He snorted as he crossed his arms across his chest.

"Yeah, well that illegal way was what I did to make sure you could have what you needed!"

"You know, I'm sick of you constantly throwing in my face what you did for me. Shit, I didn't ask you to do it now did I?" he questioned.

"No, but you damn sure didn't turn it down either!" I shot back at his ass.

Ethan started laughing and shaking his head, which pissed me off even more. I was two seconds from taking that fucking griddle I just cooked on, and bash that shit across his head.

"I tell you what, how much do I owe you, so I won't have to hear about this shit again? Shit, how much do I owe yo brother's too?" Ethan asked as he pushed his chair away from the table.

I stood there, at the island for a few seconds, and just stared at his ass. I was beginning to really develop a hate for Ethan. Not only was he acting like he just didn't give a fuck about us anymore, but he was also acting as if he was better than me. I refused to sit around and let Ethan think that he was I was some shit on the bottom of his shoe, all while his ass was running with different bitches every day. Honestly, I wasn't even sure if my husband still loved me, but he was going to respect me.

"Look Ethan, I'm not trying to argue with you baby, and I'm sorry for coming at you like that. I just want us to spend some time together that's all. You know I love when we go out together and loosen up for a bit. That's why I suggested us going to the club together tonight for a while. We don't have to stay long. Besides, there might be some new potential clients there. You know how these athletes like to be on the scene when someone big in the streets throws a party in the club." I said in a calmer tone.

I knew my last statement about potential clients would have him thinking. Ethan wasn't trying to turn no type of money down. My purpose was to get back on Ethan good side, so that I can turn these tables back around, and have control again.

Pushing his chair back to the table, he pulled his plate back in front of him, and resumed eating before answering me.

"Fine, Chase. We can go out tonight, but I'm only going to scope out the scene to see who's in the building, and then I'm out. If you wanna stay behind and party with the rest of the hood rats, then that's on you." Ethan spoke.

I started biting on the inside of my cheeks, preventing me from responding to the bullshit that had just came out of his mouth. I knew Ethan was testing me, and expected me to react, but I refused to...at least not this time. Tonight, I planned on looking like I had just stepped off the run way at New York fashion week, with my sexy ass husband next to me, get his ass pissy drunk, and then, bring him home and fuck him like my life depended on it. I already had the babysitter on stand bye, just in case Ethan was adamant on not coming with me tonight.

Once he was done eating, Ethan left the table, and out the kitchen without saying anything else to me. It was really starting to bother me with the way he was treating me. Ethan acted as if I some bum bitch who was getting on his nerves, instead of the woman who has been by his side through it all. Getting up from the table myself, I grabbed the plates, and straightened back up the kitchen.

When I was done, I headed upstairs to take a shower, so that I could hit the boutiques, and find something to wear for tonight. Although I had two closets full of clothes, with the majority of them with tags still attached to them, I still brought something new whenever I was going out. Walking into our bedroom, I heard the shower running in the bathroom. I walked over to Ethan side of the bed, and noticed his phone lying on the night stand face down.

Picking up the phone, I saw that he had the lock code on it; which wasn't unusual. Right when I was about to put it back down, it chimed. Since the phone was locked, I could only see part of the message pop up on the home screen, with the name Kennedi. Whoever this Kennedi was, sent a heart emoji to Ethan phone. I immediately tried to unlock his phone, so that I could see the text messaging thread between the both of them, but after trying my birthday and then Imani's, and both still not being the right codes, I put that phone back face down.

I went around to my side of the bed, and sat down. Fuming, I had to know who the fuck was this Kennedi bitch, and why was she sending my husband a fucking heart emoji?

CHAPTER 6

Kennedi

"Hello?" I answered with a smile as I pulled into one of the available parking spaces. When I don't hear anything, I turn the volume up on my radio, which is Bluetooth connected to my phone. "Hello. Ethan, are you there?" I frown picking up my phone to see if he'd somehow got disconnected.

"Yeah...yeah, I'm here, babe," he finally spoke. "I'm sorry, but my secretary had stepped into my office and I had to handle something really quick."

"No biggie. I just thought that the phone had hung up," I told him, glad to hear his voice. "Other than being your normal busy self, what are you up to?"

"Thinking about you," Ethan responded causing my heart to skip a beat.

"Is that so?" I blushed immediately feeling like I a high school girl with a crush. "What exactly have you been thinking about?"

"Do you want the smooth answer, or do you want the truth?"

"I always want the truth," I told him, meaning every word. "But you can add a little bit of smooth if you like."

"Well, I've been thinking about us. I know we haven't known each other long, but I already miss everything about you. I miss your smile, the way the sun bounces off of your eyes, and even the way you smell," he revealed, "I feel crazy saying this out loud, but I haven't even washed the t-shirt I let you wear when we were together because it smells just like you. I know I sound like a sucka saying something like that—"

"No, you don't," I cut him off. Reaching into my purse, I grabbed a tube of my lip-gloss and twisted off the top. "You sound like a man who likes a woman. There's nothing wrong with that." I paused as I pulled down my visor and glided the brush across each of my lips. "I actually think it's sweet."

"Good," Ethan chuckled, "I didn't want you to think that I was weird or nothing like that."

After sharing a laugh, I told him, "Truthfully, I've been thinking about you as well."

"Care to share?"

"I've just been thinking that it would be cool if we lived closer to one another," I told him sliding the lip-gloss back inside my bag. "With you up in New York, and me all the way down here in Savanna, who knows when we'll get a chance to see each other again. I liked hanging out with you."

"I know our situation isn't ideal right now, but I know we'll figure something out," Ethan promised, "How long has it been since we've seen one another, two weeks right?"

"Yeah, about two weeks," I agreed.

"Hmmm, let me think," he paused, "How about I come down next weekend and stay for a few days? That way you can show me around Georgia, and we can spend a little more time together."

I can't keep the smile off of my even if I tried. "I think that would be a great idea."

"Well, it's settled. I'll have my secretary book me a flight and a car, and I will be there next Friday."

"I'm looking forward to it." I beamed.

"Alright, well I'm sorry, babe, but I gotta go," Ethan sighed, "I have a meeting in less than an hour and it's downtown, so I have to hurry out of here. We'll talk later, alright?"

"OK." I replied, "You drive safe."

"I'm definitely going to try."

"You better. See ya."

"See ya."

Once we disconnect the call, I killed my engine, and allowed my head to rest against the seat. Thoughts of Ethan clouded my mind and all I can do is shake my head. It amazes me how quickly that someone can start to have feelings for a person. It's only been about three weeks since we first met, but I'd be lying if I said that he didn't cross my mind at least a few times a day. No doubt it's nice to know that I cross his as well. Just thinking about what he said about not washing his shirt that I wore has me cheesing hard as hell. It's little things like that that makes me like Ethan more and more each time we speak. He really does know how to make a woman feel special, and it all started that night that we met in Miami.

While sitting at the bar chit chatting like we were old friends, it was then that I got a chance to know, Ethan McKenzie, a bit more. I found out that he was an only child, who was born and raised in Springfield, Missouri. At the age of fifteen, both of his parents were killed in a plane crash, which resulted in him having to relocate to Chicago to live with his grandmother. A mere two years later, tragedy struck his family once again when she too was taken away from him by cancer; leaving Ethan alone in the world. Although I didn't really know him at that time, I remember placing my hand on his shoulder, because I could see the hurt on his face when he spoke about his deceased family members. I wanted Ethan to know that even though I was a stranger, I was compassionate enough to be there for him if he needed me.

Soon after, we lightened the mood and switched the subject up a bit to a more of our corporate lives. After telling Even about how my company came to be, he immediately praised me for turning my social media fame, into something beneficial to my future. It was then that he revealed that he was the owner of a very prestigious company. I swear my mouth dropped to my chest when he told me that he was the creator of McKenzie Management. To know that he was the face of the company that did work with many of the top paid athletes; some of whom I work with as well was mind blowing. We continued our chat until it was time for the restaurant to close. Soon, we both called it a night, but not before we exchanged numbers.

The following day, Ethan called to ask if he could take me to lunch. Since I had such a good time with him the evening before, I accepted. Due to the fact that we were staying at the same hotel, I expected him to just meet me in the front lobby. Instead, he asked for my room number, and not long after I gave it to him, he showed up at my door with a dozen long stem red roses. That in itself was something new to me because I had never received flowers from anyone other than my daddy. Hell, Darnell had never even thought to do something like that. After I thanked Ethan and put the flowers in water, we headed out to eat. With me not really

55

being familiar with Miami, I allowed Ethan to pick the place. We ended up going to this restaurant called, Kush. There I had one of the best sandwiches that I had ever had in my entire life! It was called; *Grandpa Joe's Pastrami Reuben* and it was delicious. I remember Ethan laughing at me for eating so fast because I finished way before him. I didn't even care though because it was that good.

Once we finished eating, Ethan took me to the different places in Miami that I had never seen before. We went to the Seaquarium, and to Bayfront Park before finally settled at the beach, where we had a picnic and watched the sunset. There we spoke about more of our lives, and it was then that I found out he had a daughter named Imani. Immediately my guard went up because while I was having fun with him, I did not want to be involved with someone who was already involved with someone else. Apparently, Ethan noticed the change in my demeanor, because he quickly let me know that he was no longer with his ex-wife and that they had been divorced for more than two years. He promised that all they did was co-parent and nothing more. While I heard him and hoped that he wasn't lying, I still kept my guard up, because you just never know. While he didn't have the normal tan line on his ring finger, men were tricky these days and found better ways to hide it. I wasn't going to be the fool, because

I'd just gotten out of a toxic relationship, and didn't plan on jumping back into another one; especially being someone's damn mistress. Nonetheless, we continued our evening, before we parted

ways.

Coincidentally, the following day was the day that we both were to depart from Miami, and neither of us really wanted to go. While I was thinking it, Ethan was the first to actually speak up. He asked me if I was willing to stay a few more days, and since I didn't have any work to do back home, I agreed to stay. I wasn't really trying to rush home to deal with Darnell and his nonsense anyway, so I was glad to stay a bit longer. This made Ethan very happy, so happy that he offered to pay for my hotel stay, as well as for everything else I may need while in Miami, including my flight back. While I was grateful for his offer, I politely declined, informing him—in a nice way—that it was not necessary. I wanted him to know that I made my own money and could afford to pay my own tabs; which was something that my parents had always instilled in me. Those few days turned into a full week. While there we went sightseeing, ate good food, and partied with some of his boys that Ethan knew that resided there. I can honestly say that I had a blast, and was happy that I stayed.

It's been two weeks since I've been back home, and Ethan and I have stayed in constant contact. He calls or texts me numerous times a day to see how I'm doing, and we spend most of our nights on the phone. I still have my guard up a little, because I really don't know what to expect with his baby mother issue, but the fact that he's always so available to me makes the fact that he says they are not together more believable. Either way, I'm going to keep an eye out just to make sure that I don't get hurt in the process. When I asked Tasha was I being paranoid, she simply told me to keep my eyes and ears open, because you just never know. I'm going to make sure that I follow her advice because I'm not trying to get my heart broken again. For now, I'm happy and looking forward to seeing him when he comes down next week. I plan to take him to a few places here like he did for me while we were in Miami.

Gathering my things, I drop my phone into my purse, and exit my car, hitting the alarm before making my way towards Kroger. I'm tired of eating out and plan to cook myself a nice dinner tonight, but with an empty fridge, that seemed next to impossible. While I walk, I mentally prepare a grocery list in my head; which is something that I should have done before I even left my apartment. As soon as my hands touch the cart, my text message alert goes off. After maneuvering myself out of anyone's way, I dig into my bag in search for my phone. When I have it in my hand, I unlock it and immediately annoyance is etched on my face.

MOOK: *I know you can see that I've been calling that fucking phone! I've been trying to be nice and give you some time, but you taking this shit too far! Stop fucking playing with me man, and talk to a nigga. Don't make me do a pop up at ya crib again, like I used to do before. Call me AS SOON as you get this.*

"Ugh!" I sighed rolling my eyes. "Get a fucking life."

I'm not sure why, but Darnell still doesn't seem to get that I'm done with him and his bullshit. I haven't' spoken to him since the day I left for Miami, yet he continues to call or text me at least three times a day. Maybe it's because I've said that I was done with him more times than I can count, only to turn around and let him right back into my life as well as my bed. Whatever the reason, he's going to have to understand that things are over between the two of us. I'm moving on this time, and he should do the same.

Just thinking about him and his threat to 'pop up' has me nervous about Ethan coming down to visit. I don't want him to think that I have a bunch of drama going on in my life, so I plan to keep Darnell as far away from my apartment as I possibly can. The wheels of my mind start to turn and an idea pops into my head. I begin to think that a hotel stay would be a perfect solution. That way I don't have to worry about Darnell dropping by in the middle of the night and ruining everything like I know he would. Truthfully, I just wish that he would leave me the hell alone, but that's easier said than done. Making my way into the grocery store, I can't help but think that Darnell is going to make shit hard for me and Ethan. I just hope that all of his nonsense doesn't run my new boo away, before things even really get started.

CHAPTER 7

Chace

"Fuck, now how in the hell am I going to hide this shit?" I said as I stared at my neck in mirror.

"I don't know bitch, but you better think of something quick before Ethan kill yo ass!" my home girl, Tricia burst out laughin g as she blew smoke out from the weed we were smoking on.

I came by Tricia house for a while today, to feel her in on my latest drama, before I had to pick Imani up from dance practice. I'll be glad when Patricia brings her ass back from Mexico, because this shit with picking Imani up, and taking her to her activities, was cutting into my free time. Patricia claimed her cousin died, so Ethan let her take two weeks off. Of course, I didn't find that shit out until this morning when she didn't show up for work. She knew to go to him with the bullshit instead of me, because I wouldn't have given a damn, and would have still told her ass to come into work. Besides, I'm sure that her ass has fifty more damn cousins running around, so one dying shouldn't matter.

Anyways, I wanted to fill Tricia in on what happened when Ethan and I went to the club the other night.

"So, how was the club? I know that shit was popping."

Tricia asked as she got comfortable on her bed.

"Girl, my brothers had that shit exclusive with bottles everywhere, and all the VIP sections on lock, but, you would have known that already if your ass been there." I rolled my eyes.

Tricia was supposed to also be at the club that night, but called me at the last minute, saying she was meeting up with some dude she was fucking with instead, so that he could drop some cash on her.

"Stop being salty boo, you know when money calls, I most definitely have to answer. Besides, I need all the coins I can get, since I plan on opening up this beauty salon. Although I have been asking my best bitch to go into business with me." She stated giving me a side look.

"What you want, is for me to put up all the money." I reminded her ass.

"It's called investing Chace, you front the money and get it back to you once the business is off the ground. You know I got the skills in this hair game, I'm just tired of working in other bitche's shop and outside of my house." Tricia frowned.

We had been having this conversation since the first-time Tricia came to me with opening up her own salon, three months ago. It was true, Tricia can do some hair, and is very well known for it' amongst other things. My girl can hook your shit up. But, Tricia also had the reputation for fucking with dudes, and then have them set up to be robbed.

The only reason she can walk around and not be fucked with in these streets, is because of who I am, and she's known to be my friend.

After I had my brothers stop this one nigga from beating her ass, when me and her were out on day, they made it clear that Tricia was not to be fucked with, long as she was with me. I did ask her on numerous occasions, when I heard rumors, if they were true about her setting these dudes up, but Tricia always denied it.

It was just too much of a coincidence, that every time she dealt with someone, they would get robbed. I knew she had enough sense not to fuck with me, because I would surely have that hoe head on a platter, and display it in the middle of Manhattan, but I still didn't want to tie my money up with her ass. I knew how the game went. Tricia may be able to do some good ass hair, but once word got out that she had her own shop now, these niggas with the deep pockets will make sure that they won't allow their females to spend money in a shop ran by Tricia.

That's why she goes from shop to shop, because if she stays at one shop too long, she starts to lose clients. Also, her fucking mouth is reckless. As a last resort, Tricia does hair out of her house; but soon as the housing authority gets word of her making extra income, and not reporting it, she is threatened with eviction.

Tricia was a hood rat all the way, but the only reason I really fucked with her, is because at a drop of a dime, I knew that she didn't mind getting her hands dirty. She was also a fun person to go clubbing with, and get the latest gossip from.

Overall, she was the cool home girl you kept at an arm length distance, and dealt with from time to time. But, going into business with? Hell no.

"We'll talk about that later." I brushed her off as I took the blunt out of her hand, and took a pull from it.

"Whatever, you always say that shit. Anyways, finish with what happened the other night."

"Girl, like I said, that shit was lit! When me and Ethan walked in, of course all eyes were on us. Those hoes were drooling over my man and niggas stayed trying to cut their eyes at me. When we got to the VIP section, that's when the real fun began with us drinking, and getting fucked up; well at least I did. Ethan ass was just sitting there, acting as if he didn't want to be there, and constantly texting on his damn phone." I said in frustration as I thought back to that night.

"Chace, now you know your husband ain't with the club scene." Tricia laughed.

Ignoring her comment, I continued.

"So, as the night went on, I was enjoying myself with dancing, and interacting with people. I was buzzed, and feeling good, until Jerome showed up with some tired ass bitch, who looked like she had on a dress from Rainbow." I shook my head.

When I saw Jerome come into our section with that chick, I tried so hard not to show my jealously. I mean, I was there with my husband, who wasn't paying my ass any attention. Then when the chick started grinding her ass all on Jerome dick, I wanted to snatch that bitch by her nappy ass tracks, and beat the fuck out of her. Jerome knew that it was bothering me, because every chance he got, he would cut his eye over at me and smirk.

"Damn Chace, you tripping on Jerome being there with some other bitch, but you were there with your man." Tricia pointed out.

I didn't like the way she said that shit, but I let it slide for now.

"And? You know I don't give a fuck! Jerome knew I was gonna be there, and for him to show up with some other bitch was straight trying me. Since Jerome felt the need to bring *extra company* with him, I decided to show his ass what time it was, and started dancing all up on Ethan, and put on a show. All eyes were on us, and I caught Jerome staring at me with a pissed off look on his face." I said laughing as I thought back to the way he was looking that night.

"Ethan caught wind of all the dudes looking at me, so he whispered in my ear that he was ready to go. In my mind, I'm thinking he was turned on from all the grinding I was doing on his dick, and wanted to go home and fuck my brains out! Before leaving the club, I excused myself, and went to the restroom. Girl, right when I came outside of the stall, I see Jerome ass standing in the ladies' room, by the door. Before I could say anything, he rushed my ass, bent me over the sink, and started tearing this pussy up from the back." I licked my tongue out as I high fived Tricia.

Thinking back to how Jerome was tearing this pussy up, caused me to get wet. I was so horny that night off the liquor, that I didn't even notice when Jerome started sucking on my neck, which I later discovered left passion marks on there.

"Bitch, I cannot believe you fucked that nigga while your husband was in the same club. I swear you are one bold chick!" Tricia stated shaking her head.

"It was obviously the liquor got the best of me that night, because I would have never done that. But I do admit, that shit was good and spontaneous." I boasted as I turned back around and looked at my neck again the mirror.

"After we were done, we both quickly washed up; Jerome unlocked the bathroom door, and we went back like nothing ever happened; but separately of course." I assured.

"Well, you need to make sure that you keep makeup on that passion mark, and try to stay clear of Ethan for a while until it disappears." Tricia suggested.

That won't be hard since he's barely home now. I thought to myself as I went inside my purse, pulled out my MAC concealer, and started dabbing it on my neck. No matter how many times Jerome and I messed around, it still picked at me in the back of my mind, how fucked up my marriage is. Don't get me wrong, I love my husband, but I also love the thrill of having whoever else I wanted. But now, it is actually starting to bother me that Ethan isn't bringing his ass home. Looking in the mirror, I grinned when I saw that the concealer had indeed covered up my indiscretion.

CHAPTER 8

Kennedi

"What do you want to get into today?" I asked Ethan when he walked passed me coming out of the bathroom. He had just taken his morning shower and was clad in nothing but a pair of pajama pants.

"I don't know. I think I'll leave that up to you. You're the guide," he responded as he climbed back into the bed, pulled the sheet over his body and rolled over onto his back. "Truthfully, for all I care, we can stay in the room all day and chill. Spending time with you was the plan from the beginning, and that's all I'm trying to do."

A smile formed on my face. He definitely knew what to say and when to say it. "That sounds like a plan to me."

The truth of the matter was that it was music to my ears. I had no clue where I would take Ethan next. He'd only been visiting for three days, and we'd already gone to the aquarium, the park, and out to eat at some of the best restaurants in my part of Georgia. After mixing in one of the local clubs, I didn't know what else to put on the agenda. Since I really don't get out much, because I work all of the time, I'm not familiar with all of the good places to go.

Thank God, Google was such a big help, otherwise, I would have been lost and we would have
never left the hotel to begin with.

"I bet, because I can tell that you were running out of places to take me," he laughed.

"I guess you're right. You ain't gotta judge though," I told him picking up one of the pillows and hitting him a few times with it.

I laughed as I watched him try unsuccessfully to dodge my hits. As I lifted the pillow over my head to strike him one more time, Ethan sat up on his elbows and grabbed me by my arms. He pulled me towards him so fast, that in an instant, we were so close that our noses were touching. The smile that was once on his face, was replaced with a different look; a look that I knew all too well. The reason being is that I wore the same exact one; a look of lust. Allowing the pillow to fall from my grasp, I just sat there breathing deeply and lost in my own thoughts. Ethan and I stared at one another for a few more moments, each trying to figure out what to do next. We both must have come to the exact same conclusion at the exact same time because seconds later the two of us leaned in and mashed our lips together. I moaned as I accepted his tongue as it snaked around in my mouth, giving him mine in return. Although we had kissed a few times before, those were nothing like this one. This time it was much different. My eyes slid shut and rolled into the back of my head, while every nerve

in my body came alive.

Ethan pulled me closer and leaned in some more, which caused me to roll over on my side. I cupped the back of his bald head, as we continued to kiss. Slowly, his hands roamed up my body, from my thighs, passed my hips and on up to my stomach. When I felt his hand slide under the lace camisole I wore and make its way towards my breast, I tensed up. While Ethan's caress felt good, I was a nervous wreck. It wasn't like I was a virgin because I was far from that. Darnell and I had had sex so many times over the years that I had lost count. This nervousness stemmed from something else, and I knew exactly what that was. As we started to get hot and heavy, I realized something. I realized that I was afraid of Ethan and I moving to the next level of this thing we had going on. What that was, I didn't even know. Up until this point, all we'd done was kiss a few times. Ethan must have sensed my apprehension because he stopped and sat up.

"Is everything okay?" he asked looking down at me with worry. "Am I moving too fast? If so, I don't mind stopping. Just say the word." He held both of his hands up.

"No, it's not you," I replied, before taking a deep breath. "It's just that I'm not the kind of girl who has sex just for sport. I like it to mean something, ya know?" I shrugged.

"This will mean somethi—" Ethan started, but I cut him off.

"Please don't say that, especially if you really don't mean it," I spoke. "I've only been in one relationship my entire life, and that was with my ex that I told you about. He was the one and only man that I've ever been with. So this here is different for me."

"You didn't have to tell me that, Kennedi. I didn't know that he was the only guy, but I could tell what kind of woman I was dealing with."

"Well, then you know that I don't just want a sexual relationship with you... or anybody else for that matter," I told him honestly. "Look, I don't know what this is that we have, but I don't want to go in thinking that it's more than what it is and mess around and get my feelings hurt. Sex has a way of complicating things, and right now I don't need any added worries."

"Then you'll be glad to know that I don't just want a sexual relationship with you either," Ethan disclosed, "I know you might think I'm just saying this because I want to sleep with you, but that's not the case. I like you, a lot,

Kennedi. I enjoy talking to you, and I love being around you even more. You don't have a clue how long I've been unhappy. That day I ran into you was like fate. At that point, I had all but giving up on love," he paused. "Not saying that I love you or anything because that would be creepy." We shared a laugh before he got serious again. "Truthfully, I didn't think it was possible to have these type of feelings again for anyone, but you're showing me that it is." Reaching out, he used his finger to lift my chin so that he could look me directly in the eyes. "I'm not sure what we have at this moment either, but I'm damn sure willing to give us a shot." Ethan smiled. "You won't know what will happen until you try."

"You're right," I agreed, "I guess I'm willing to give a shot as well." I grinned.

"You guess, huh?" He chuckled.

"You know what I mean." I mushed him on the shoulder. "I want to see what happens between us as well."

Placing his hand on my thigh he asked, "Do you think you can do the long distance thing?"

Before answering, I thought about it for a minute. I must have taken too long, because Ethan's face showed worry. "I think I can. You just have to promise me something."

"Anything." He replied.

"You have to promise me that things are over between you and your ex. I know that she's the mother of your child, but I don't want to have to worry about what you're doing with her when I'm not around."

Although Ethan and I hadn't made it official before now, I often wondered if he was with her when he was back home. Having come out of a relationship where I was cheated on numerous times, had me leery of all men. I'd be lying if I said that thoughts of Ethan with his ex-wife didn't cloud my head on more than one occasion. I had never dealt with a man who had a child before, but even I knew that things could get messy when kids were involved. Having a baby with someone is a bond that could not easily be broken; especially when that person was your wife. Other than finding out that his ex-was basically a ghetto hood rat with a terrible attitude, I didn't know much else about her other than her name, nor did I ask. I figured that that was Ethan's business, and if there was something that he wanted to share with me, he would when he felt the time was right. Until then I just hoped that he wasn't playing me.

"I promise you that you don't have anything to worry about. Chace is a thing of the past. You can trust when I tell you that there is nothing there between us," Ethan told me.

"If I could get custody of Imani, she wouldn't even be in the picture at all."

"You don't have to do all that," I spoke up, "Unless you're saying that she's a bad mother." My ears perked as I waited for his response because if he told me that she was, it would make me wonder why on Earth he would not only marry
someone like that, but have a child with them as well.

"She's not a bad mother, but she's not a good one either." He paused. "Let's just say that she turned out to not be the woman that I thought she was. I guess you can say that she put up a good front."

"Well, I'm sorry you had to go through whatever she put you through."

"Thanks, but enough about her." Ethan glanced over at me. "Do you want to go out and grab something to eat, or do you just want to order something?"

"We can do that later," I licked my lips, "Right now I want to finish what we started."

"Is that righ—" Before he had a chance to finish his sentence, my leaned in and covered his mouth with mine.

This time it was me who leaned in and took the lead. Placing my hand on his bare chest, I nudged him just a little bit, letting him know that I wanted him to lie down. Once

Ethan was lying on his back, I broke our kiss, sat completely up and straddled his midsection. He looked up at me with a smirk, before he traced his bottom lip with his tongue. *He's so damn sexy,* I thought to myself, as I lean down and kissed him again; this time more aggressive than before. When I felt his hands travel up my body and reach my camisole, I didn't stop him; instead, I assisted him in removing it. Reaching down, I grabbed the bottom of the lace fabric from his grasp, and pulled it over my head, revealing my bra-less breast. The cool breeze coming from the air conditioner caused my nipples to immediately stand at attention. I moaned when Ethan lifted up and placed my left one into his mouth. As he swirled his tongue around it and tugged at it gently with his teeth, I closed my eyes and threw my head back.

Ethan used that as his chance to take over and rolled me onto my back. After standing up, he grabbed my ankles, pulled me to the edge of the bed, and leaned down between my legs. Soon, I felt him began to kiss the inner parts of my thighs. Placing his arms under my hips, he tugged at the bottom of my shorts until they and my underwear were both completely off. My breath got caught in my throat when I felt his tongue graze my southern lips. I was scared, yet excited. In all of the years that I'd been with Darnell, he had never gone down on me before. He used to claim that it was nasty but always expected me to put his dick in my mouth. I had done it a few times because I loved to please him, but after I realized that he wasn't going to do me; I stopped that shit. Hell, that may have been one of the reasons why he had constantly cheated on me. He'd probably found someone who would do the things that I would no longer do.

"Ahhhh," I whimpered when I felt Ethan part my lips with

his tongue. Seconds later, he wrapped his entire mouth around my pearl and gently sucked on it.

As I laid on the bed lost in the pleasurable feeling that I was receiving, I couldn't do anything but cry out. It felt so fucking good, and I honestly couldn't put it into words even if I tried. Definitely one of the best sensations that I'd ever experienced, and feeling it now made me wish that I had gotten it done sooner. *Stupid ass Darnell.* I guess you never really know what you're missing if you've never had it. Ethan continued to alternate in licking and sucking until my body was damn near having convulsions. After he finished making love to my kitty orally, he sat up and looked down me, as my legs continued to shake and shudder. I had never come so hard in my life, and laying there trembling like a damn fool was embarrassing as hell, but I quickly got over it!

My chest heaved up and down, as my breathing slowly returned to normal. Clad in absolutely nothing, I scooted back and sat up myself. Reaching out, I gestured for Ethan to join me on the bed, and he did. With him now directly in front of me, I pulled him closer and traced his lips with my tongue, tasting my own juices.

"Taste good, don't it?" he asked. I nodded my head, before slipping my tongue into his now parted lips.

Breaking our kiss, I looked up at him. "Do you want me to return the favor?"

"Maybe later," he replied, "I'm ready to see just how good you feel inside."

Ethan reached down and placed his arm across my lower back. Picking me up slightly, he moved me back to the top of the bed, before laying me down. I watched him lustfully as he stood up and slid his pajama pants off, before he kicked across the room. Leaning over, he reached into the nightstand on his side of the bed, grabbed his wallet, and retrieved a gold condom wrapped. When he sat up to roll it on, I caught of glimpse of what he was working with and got nervous all over again. Don't get me wrong, Ethan wasn't King Ding-a-ling or anything like that, but he was larger than what I was accustomed too. With Darnell, it always felt like I was being stretched to capacity, so I was kind of worried about how Ethan's would feel.

"Don't worry, I'm going to take it slow," he promised as if he was reading my mind.

Biting down on my bottom lip, I exhaled ready to get started. Ethan leaned down and licked my right nipple, before pulling it into his mouth completely. I closed my eyes, and moaned, feeling his lower body touch mine. When I felt something trace my lower lips, I tensed up, preparing for him to enter me, but he didn't right away. Instead, he slid the head up and down my slit, teasing me every time he applied pressure to my already sensitive clit. Other than our breathing, the sound of my juices was the only other thing that could be heard. Moments later, when I was dripping wet, and begging him to give it to me, Ethan pushed the head in. I tensed up and put my hand on his chest to prevent him from going any futher. It had been months since Darnell and I had had sex because I refused to sleep with him knowing that he was possibly fucking someone else. For that reason, I was more than a little tight.

As promised, Ethan took his time. Once I gave him the okay to continue, he slowly inched himself into me little by little. When he was all the way inside, we sealed the deal and officially took our relationship to the next level.

Make Sure She Knows About Me

CHAPTER 9

Chace

"Mommy, when is my daddy coming home?" Imani asked me for what seemed like the tenth time.

"I don't know Imani, and I wish you stop asking me all these damn questions about your precious daddy! Why don't you call him and ask him!" I snapped as I cut the blender on to finish making my strawberry daiquiri.

It was Saturday afternoon, after one o'clock, and Imani and I had both recently just gotten up. Normally, she would be up early on the weekends to have her so-called *daddy daughter day* with her father, but since the muthafucka ain't here, I just let her ass sleep in with me. Especially since Patricia still hasn't returned from Mexico yet. Imani climbed down from the bar stool at the kitchen counter where she was coloring, and walked out of the kitchen. Minutes later, she came back with her iPhone in her hand, as she sat back down at the counter.

Moments later, I heard her giggling into the phone.

"Hi daddy!" she greeted.

I cut my eyes over at her and my blood instantly started boiling. It's amazing how quickly Ethan picks up the phone when he sees Imani calling him, but I've been calling his ass since last night, and he has yet to answer for me. I know this sounds crazy, but the relationship between my daughter and her father sickens me. Ethan shows so much love and affection towards Imani, that it reminds me of how he used to be that way with me.

I know Imani is Ethan's world, but hell, I'm the one that brought her into this muthafucka, so that should count for something! As she sat there and continued to have conversation with her daddy, I became more pissed, so much so that I snatched the phone out of her hand.

"Oh, so can answer for Imani, but not me?" I yelled into the phone, interrupting him in the middle of whatever it was he was saying to Imani.

"What's up, Chace." Ethan sighed.

His whole tone changed just that quick once he knew I was on the phone. This bastard didn't even try to hide the fact that he didn't want to talk to me.

"What's up?" I repeated as I took the phone away from my ear and looked at it.

"What's up is that you haven't been home Ethan, and when I call you, your ass doesn't answer my calls!" I was so pissed, that if he had been in my face right now, I swear I would try to knock this nigga in his shit!

"I'm working Chace, you know this." Was all he offered

as an excuse.

"So, you working stops you from checking on your wife and child back at home?   What if something happened?"

"Imani can always call her daddy if something is wrong." He replied.

I could not believe how nonchalant Ethan was being about all this.

"You know what Ethan, it's mighty funny how big and bad you've been acting lately. The sudden out of town trips, not answering my calls or texts, and when you are home, you're locked up in your office. It doesn't take a blonde bitch to understand that you got some new pussy. Hell, this pussy must be good, but let me warn you, *when* I find out about what the fuck you have going on, because I will find out, it's lights out for you and that bitch Kennedi!" I blurted out.

I could tell that he was caught off guard with me mentioning that name, because he got quiet. I still remembered that Kennedi text in his phone with the heart emoji. It didn't take a genius to figure out, that was who he was probably fucking around with this time. But just like the others, I'll get rid of this bitch too.

"What did you just say?" Ethan finally spoke.

"I see that got your attention. Ethan, fuck you and that bitch. Like I said, when I find out who she is, I'm fucking the both of ya'll up!" I screamed into the phone, and ended the call before he could say anything else.

I slid Imani phone back to her over the counter, as she sat there with her mouth open looking at me.

"Imani why are you sitting there, staring at me like that for?" I yelled annoyed.

"Because mommy, you're always so mean to daddy." she had the nerve to mumble under her breath.

She might have thought I didn't hear that shit, but I caught it.

"Fuck yo' daddy! Matter of fact, take your grown ass to your room until I feel like seeing you again!" I ordered.

Imani quickly grabbed her phone off the counter, and hurried out the kitchen. I finished making my daiquiri and poured it into the glass. When I was finished, I went into the entertainment room, and grabbed the remote to catch up on my shows. I started with Marriage boot camp. I swear Benzino needed to leave that hoe Althea alone. As I was sipping on my drink and watching my show, my phone vibrated. I grabbed it off the side table and saw that I had a text message.

ETHAN: *If you ever talk like that in front of my daughter again we gone have some problems.*

ME: *We already have problems dumb ass!*

ETHAN: *No, you have the problem, I'm good. Lol*

I'm glad he thought that this was the game. We'll see who'll be laughing once I get through with his ass. Right when I got ready to respond, Jerome text me.

JEROME: *WYD (what you doing)*

ME: *Sitting home relaxing*

JEROME: *I feel like getting in some pussy, let me slide through.*

ME: *Slide through? How you know my husband ain't home?*

JEROME: *Man that nigga ain't never home! LOL (laughing out loud) What's up?*

I sat there for a while contemplating. Ethan was acting an ass, and thought this shit was a game. Suddenly, I had the urge to get back at Ethan in the most hurtful way possible, and I knew just how to start by doing that.

ME: *OK, you can come over but my daughter is here.*

JEROME*: Shit put her lil ass up in her room while I knock her momma off.*

ME*: Lmao (laughing my ass off) boy you stupid! Just bring yo' ass on*

JEROME*: Bet. I'll be there in an hour.*

I downed the rest of my drink, cut the TV off, and headed upstairs. I walked into Imani room to find her on her iPad with her Beats over her ears.

"Imani!" I yelled loud to get her attention.

"Yes mommy?" she answered taking her earphones off.

"I'm about to have grown up company, so I need for you to stay in your room until they leave. I'll come get you when I'm done."

"But what if I get thirsty or hungry?" she asked.

"Then I suggest you take your ass downstairs right now, and get you something to eat and snack on until I tell you to come out this room!" I barked.

Normally Imani isn't allowed to eat or drink in her room, because of her white carpet, but due to these circumstances she getting a pass. She got up, and ran past me downstairs to get what she needed out of the kitchen. I walked across the hall to my bedroom where I jumped in the shower for a quick wash and touch-up shave. Once I was done, I lathered myself in my diamonds body lotion, put on a lace bra and panty set, and put my robe on to cover it up. Right when I was finishing up, I received a text from Jerome telling me that he was outside.

Time to get this kitty taken care of I grinned as I got up, and headed downstairs.

Before I went to let Jerome in, I went back by Imani's room to check on her. I opened her door, to see that she was back on her IPad, with her headphones over her ear again eating on an apple. *Good.* I hurried downstairs to let Jerome in. Soon as I opened the door, I looked out making sure that no one saw him as I ushered him inside.

"Come on, follow me and be quiet because Imani is in her room." I instructed him as I grabbed a hold of his hand, and led him up the stairs towards my bedroom that I shared with my husband.

Soon as we stepped inside, I closed the door and locked it. I went over to the fireplace and grabbed the remote to turn the TV on as I cut the volume up loud enough to drown out our voices. Jerome took a seat at the foot of the bed and started taking his clothes off. I stood in front of him and untied my robe letting it drop to the floor displaying my sexiness.

"Damn girl." He said as he grabbed on my waist and pulled me to him.

He started kissing on my stomach as he pulled my breast out of my bra. Putting my right breast into his mouth, he began to suck on it, then switched to biting on it; just like I like it.

"Hmm" I moaned as I leaned my head back.

While sucking on my breast, Jerome reached down with his free hand, and started massaging my pussy through the crotch of my panties. I was so soaked, that my juices were sliding down my thighs.

"Take this shit off and jump on this dick," he commanded as he slapped my ass.

I slid out of my panties, as Jerome took off the rest of his clothes, and leaned all the way back on the bed stroking his dick waiting on me.

My mouth watered as I looked on at him jacking his dick. I was about to fuck this nigga into another dimension. Not only was I about to get the satisfaction of fucking him, but the fact that it was in the bed I shared with my husband is a bonus!

Chapter 10

Kennedi

It was the morning that Ethan was due to return home, and I had been dreading it since yesterday. As we laid in the bed after having sex, I just stared at the ceiling lost in my own thoughts. He has only been here with me for a few days, and I was already used to having him around. I hated to see Ethan go but knew that he had to. He had a life back in New York that he had to get back to, and that life included his daughter. While I knew I was going to miss him, it was selfish of me to want to keep him with me, knowing that he had a little girl who missed him even more than I did.

Reaching up, I wiped the sweat off of my forehead and sighed. *Could I really do this long distance relationship thing?* It was something that I really needed to know. It all sounded good to say, but would it actually be something that I could do? Would phone calls, texts, and FaceTime be enough to hold me over until the next time Ethan and I got a chance to see one another? I wasn't sure, but I hoped that it would because I liked him, a lot.

"What's on your mind?" Ethan asked rolling over on his side to look at me.

"Nothing, just thinking about the fact that you have to

leave today," I replied.

"You know if I could stay longer, I would."

"I know." I nodded. "I'm not tripping on that. It's just that I'm going to miss you." My bottom lip poked out and I stared at him with sad eyes.

Sitting up, Ethan scooted back up against the headboard. "I'm sure it won't be as much as I'll miss you," he said looking down at me. This caused me to smile.

"Why do you always know the perfect time to say the the best things?"

He shrugged. "I'm not sure. I guess I just say how I feel when I feel it."

Lifting myself into a sitting position, I leaned over and climbed on top of Ethan's lap, straddling him. With my arms placed on each of his shoulders, I lean in until my bare breast touched his chest. Gripping the back of his head, I pulled him into a kiss. When we were finished, I leaned back and just stared at him.

"We're going to be okay aren't we?" I asked looking directly in the eyes.

Ethan's forehead crinkled, as he looked at me confused. "Yeah, why you ask that?"

"I don't know." I shrugged.

"Tell me what's on your mind, beautiful," he urged.

"Well, I hate to keep bringing this up, but I worry about the situation you have with your ex-wife. I know that with children involved, things can be complicated. I've gone through a bunch of bullshit, and I'll be the first one to admit that I have trust issues, but at the same time, those issues stem from my past relationship." Removing my arms from around his neck, I drop them at my sides. "Now, don't get me wrong, because I do realize that you and Darnell are two different people, and I really want to trust you, but I also don't want to naive. This thing we have here is fresh. It hasn't even been a full month yet, so I don't expect things to be perfect between the two of us, but I also want you to know that I'm not going to just deal with anything. I may be young, but I'm far from stupid. So, if you're not sure that I am what you want, please let me know, so I won't get hurt in the process," I told him laying my cards all on the table. "I just don't want to end up with the short end of the stick.

"I know that this is a new thing for the both of us, and even with that being said, this is something that I want to try and make work," Ethan started. "You don't have to worry about Chace at all. Like I've told you before, what I had with her is dead. She may be Imani's mother, but that's pretty much it. I have no desire to deal with her, and I damn sure don't want to have sex with her. To be honest, I don't even give a shit what she does or who she does it with. That's just how serious I am. My only connection back in New York is my daughter and my business. If I could have Imani without her mother fighting me tooth and nail in the courts, I'd do just that, just so I wouldn't have to deal with Chace's bullshit anymore. I can literally run my company from anywhere." He touched my face with his hand. "So, I get that you have trust issues, but I need for you to trust me when I tell you that you have nothing to worry about," Ethan promised.

"OK." Is all I say in return.

"We can make this work. Phone calls, texts throughout the day, and talking on the phone all night. I can come here when I can, or you can come to New York." He smiled. "We can even find time to meet while working. You travel to handle things for your clients, and I do the same. I'm sure we can figure out something. We just have to try," Ethan explained. "I'm willing to if you are."

"I guess you're right." I grinned. "I never thought about it that much."

"See, ya man got you. It's been on my mind since before I came out here."

"Really?"

"Yeah, I wasn't playing when I said that I can see us being together."

I laughed. "I see."

"So," I watched as his facial expression changed to a more serious one. "do I have to worry about your ex?"

"What?" I scoffed. "No, Darnell and I are done. I haven't even spoken to him since the day I left for Miami, and I don't plan on it," I told him honestly.

"Good, because I was wondering if things had changed before I got here."

"Why you ask that?" I inquired with my head cocked to the side.

"Because we're at a hotel." Ethan raised his arms in the air and motioned them around the room. "I know that you have your own apartment, and wondered why you just didn't take me there."

I snorted and shook my head. "Well, I decided to just stay at a hotel after he sent me a text message and threatened to do a pop up at my house if I didn't call him back. I didn't want him to come over while you were there, because Lord knows he would have acted a fool. I didn't want that to happen and have you thinking that something was going on between the two of us, so I booked a room instead."

"Oh, I get it."

"Yeah, I can deal with Darnell, but I didn't want to expose you to my drama."

"Makes sense." Ethan nodded.

"Is there anything else I can help you with?" I asked with a smile.

"Yeah, you can get me some more of this good loving before I leave," he replied before he leaned over and reached into the drawer.

With a condom wrapper in his hand, he tore it open with his teeth. Once the rubber was exposed, I reached up and took it from his hand, before scooting back and rolling it down on his shaft myself. Ethan moaned as my tiny hands gripped his manhood slowly jerking him off. He responded by reaching around to grab my waist. With just his right arm, he lifted me slightly, while I used my hand to guide the head of his dick to my opening. I gasped as my body slowly slid down the length of his pole. Once I was adjusted to his size, I started to rock my hips back and forth, planning to make this last time count.

*****

Cutting off the water, I reached for the towel and climbed out of the shower. Ethan had been gone for close to an hour, and it was almost check out time, so I decided to clean up before I left. Once I had finished patting myself dry,

I lotioned my body from head to toe and began to get dressed. With all of my stuff packed into my bag, all I had to do was put my body wash, and other toiletries away. Now dressed in a flower printed maxi dress, I slid my feet into a pair of sandals and walked around the room once more to make sure that I wasn't leaving anything behind. When I was satisfied that I wasn't, I dropped my toiletry bag into my overnight bag, threw it on my shoulder and left out of the room. My next stop was to the front desk to check out.

"Good morning. I'm ready to check out of room eight-twenty-four. Name Kennedi Carter," I told the front desk clerk. I watched her as she typed away on the computer in front of her, before looking up at me.

"You're good to go, Ms. Carter. By the way, your credit card will not be charged for your stay, because it has already been paid for," she told me with a bright smile.

My eyebrows furrowed with confusion. "I'm sorry, but maybe you have the wrong room."

She looked down at the computer once more, before looking back at me.

"No, it's room eight-twenty-four. A gentleman by the name of," she paused and typed a bit more. "Ethan McKenzie took care of the entire bill before he left this morning."

"Of course he did," I laughed. "Thought something was messed up. Well, thank you so much. You enjoy the rest of your day."

"You too, Ms. Carter, and come back to see us soon," she replied as I headed through the sliding doors to my car.

Once I placed my bag into the trunk of my Audi, I climbed inside and immediately picked up my phone. As the other end rang, I stuck the key in the ignition and brought the engine to life.

"Hey you," Ethan answered.

I smiled from just hearing his voice. "Did you make it to the airport on time?" I asked.

"Yeah, they said we should be boarding in a few minutes."

"Oh okay, you could have told me that you were paying the hotel bill. Got me sitting at the front desk looking crazy when she told me that I wouldn't be charged anything," I giggled.

He chuckled, "I'm sorry, babe. I didn't think about it until I was heading out. I meant to shoot you a text, but it slipped my mind."

"I could've paid it, you know."

"I know, but I did it for you," Ethan countered. "You do know that it's okay to let me take care of you, right."

"Yeah, I guess."

"Don't guess, just allow me to," he told me. "I know that you have your own money, and I love that you do. I get it, and I'm not trying to run your life, I just want to be a man sometimes and help out. Can you let me do that?"

"I'll try," I tell him meaning it.

I was really going to try to let Ethan do his thing because I could tell that that's what he liked to do. It wasn't like I wasn't used to seeing a man pay for things that his woman wanted or needed. My father had done it for my mother for almost twenty-five years. He was always the breadwinner, who made sure that he made enough money to take care of our entire household. All my mother had to do was cook, clean, watch after me and make sure that the bills were paid on time; with the money my father provided of course. Never had I heard my dad complain about how hard he worked because he always told me that that is what real men did. So, when I got with Darnell, I thought it would be the same way, and it was for a while. He would buy me the things I needed, even though I was working, but once he got mad about something, he would always throw anything he did back in my face. After a while, I stopped letting him do things for me because I got tired of him always bringing shit back up.

"That's all that I ask." I heard Ethan say. "I gotta go, babe, their calling us to board."

"OK, you have a safe flight and call me once you get settled," I told him.

"Will do. Talk to you later." After disconnecting the call, I dropped my phone into my bag and said a silent prayer that Ethan's flight would be a safe one. When I finished, I strapped on my seat belt and pulled out of the hotel's parking lot.

It took me close to a half hour before I made it to my apartment. Climbing out of my car, I hit the lock on my trunk and grabbed my bag. I had been gone for days, and even though I enjoyed my time with Ethan, I was glad to be home. With my bag over my shoulder, I made my way up the sidewalk, and over to my building. Just as I was about to head up the stairs, I heard someone call my name. Even before I turned around, I already knew who it was. Irritation immediately set in. Quickly, I jogged to the top landing, found my door key and attempted to get to my apartment before he caught up to me, but it was no use.

"What the hell you running for?" Darnell asked as he now stood on the steps. He was breathing hard, and looking at me all crazy.

"What the hell do you want, Mook?" I snapped.

"You can tone all that smart talk down, for real. Ain't no reason to be all nasty and shit! A nigga just trying to talk to you," he said matching my tone.

I stepped back and looked him up and down. "First of all,
I can be as nasty as I want to be because I'm in front of my damn house. Second, if I wanted to talk to you, I would have called you back, but since I didn't, that should tell you something."

"Whatever, man, I'm not trying to argue with you today, Kennedi." Darnell waved me off. "I only came by to see why you'd be ignoring me like I'm the plague or some shit."

"Come on, Mook, you already know what it is, so why do you keep making me saying it?" I asked, even though I didn't wait for his response. "It's over between us. I told you this weeks ago."

"Come on, baby, you know I love you. Why you trying to play games? What you want me to beg?" he asked reaching out to touch me lightly on the arm. Normally my heartbeat would quicken, and I would have to fight the urge not to give him, but this time, I felt nothing but annoyance.

"No, I don't want you to beg. I want to leave me alone!" I yelled. "I don't want to do this anymore. Why aren't you listening to me?"

"Because the shit's no happening!" Darnell barked.

My face softened as I looked at him seriously. "Mook, it's over. I'm sorry, but I'm just over it." I wanted to say it less anger, so maybe he would hear me better. I've always heard that sometimes people shut down when you yell, so I tried a

different approach this time.

"Nah, I'm not gone accept that. I ain't did shit, and you ain't leaving me," he waved me off shaking his head.

This nigga ain't hearing shit I said. He's clearing delusional, I thought to myself.

"You don't have a choice," I insisted. "You've done me wrong for the last time, and I'm moving the hell on." The frown that Darnell now wore made me regret opening my mouth.

"What you mean you moving on? You fucking with another nigga?" he hissed.

I blew air out of my nose, mad at myself for even saying anything. "Look, I gotta go. I'm tired and ready to get in my house. You take care of yourself, Mook."

"Nah, fuck that!" he yelled grabbing my arm. "Answer the fucking question, Kennedi!"

"Get the hell off of me!" I jerked out of his grasp. "What the hell is wrong with you? You must have lost your fucking mind!"

Darnell quickly stepped up the few stairs and closed the gap between us. He was so close that our chest was almost touching. "I don't know what has gotten into yo' ass, but you better fix it. I done told you that I wasn't fucking with that girl. This here," He pointed back and forth between the two of us. "ain't over until we both agree that it is. So, you can go ahead in that apartment of yours and do whatever it is that you gotta do, but I know one thing. You better answer the phone the next time I call."

"And if I don't?" I challenged.

"You already know how I can get, Kennedi. Don't make me take it there," he warned.

"Whatever."

"Yeah, I hear ya." Darnell smirked. "Where the hell you coming from anyway?" he asked as he looked down at the overnight bag that was over my shoulder. It was the same one that I used to bring to his house when I spent the night, so I already knew what he was thinking.

I cocked my head to the side. "Minding my business."

"Alright, Kennedi. Keeping playing games with me if you want. You gone see just how serious this shit can get."

"Bye Mook," I dismissed him, before turning around and sticking my key into the door.

"You gone head and handle your business. I'll talk to you later," He told me jogging down the steps.

"I wouldn't count on it," I mumbled as I stepped into my apartment.

Closing the door behind me, I locked it and went over to the window. When I did, I saw that Darnell was now inside his truck, and pulling away from the curb. As he drove off, all I could do was roll my eyes. This is not how I pictured things going between us. I always knew that he would try to get me to stay with him once I broke it off, but never did I think that he would resort to threats. I always knew that Darnell always had anger issues, because he would yell and act a fool. Never in the five years that we'd been together had he put his hands on me, but watching the way he acted on my steps a few minutes ago made me wonder what he was capable of. I couldn't put my finger on it, but something was definitely different about him. All I want to do is move on, but it looks like Darnell is not going to let me. I just pray that he doesn't do anything stupid because I already tell that things are getting ugly.

Reaching into my bag, I pull out my cell phone. I have to call my bestie and let her know about her crazy ass brother.

CHAPTER 11

Chace

Today, we were hosting our annual fourth of July picnic at our house. Normally, my brother's world rent out the entire park, and have it there, but this year, I wanted to have it our house instead. When I announced to Ethan that we would be having the cookout here this year, I expected his ass to give me grief about it. Instead, he was on board with us hosting it, which was shocking.

Ever since that day I cursed his ass out on the phone, and mentioned that bitch Kennedi name, Ethan has tried to do a complete turnaround, with being home more, and attentive to me.

The problem with that it is, I know that it's not genuine. Listen, a woman knows her man, especially her husband. Each time I busted Ethan on his shit, he would try and be the doting husband. Thinking, that will make me forget about the shit he has done, but I never forget. Then, when I attempt to put my guards down, that's when he goes back to his old ways. I wasn't new to this game with his ass, that's why I always took advantage of him when we were on these terms; just like I did when I decided to host the cookout this year.

Ethan hates it when there are lot of people at our house,

especially my brother's friends.

"Patricia, can you make sure that the party rental people knows that the tents are to go up in the center of the backyard, and not in the corners?" I asked, as I put the potatoe salad that I had just finished making, in the refrigerator.

Besides shopping and making money, the other thing I loved to do was cook. Since my momma ran the streets all the time, I had no choice but to learn how to cook for my brothers and me. As time went on, I got better and better, and prided on other people bragging on how good I was in the kitchen. So, for the past two days, I've been cooking my sides, and seasoning my meat.

My uncle Bud, my momma brother, was going to be responsible for grilling the meat. Only because my brothers planned on being drunk, and on the dominoes table, and Ethan planned on doing the same. Looking over at the clock on the stove, I saw that it was two in the afternoon. The cookout was scheduled to start at four. Leaving out of the kitchen, I headed upstairs to get ready. Passing by Imani room, I saw her trying on outfits in her full figure mirror. I swear for her to be only seven years old, she still took after me in being a little diva.

I always instilled in my child, that her appearance on the outside is very important.

Every time I take Imani shopping for clothes and shoes, I make her try each piece on, then evaluate it while she's wearing it; making sure it fits her body type just right. I know at being seven, that a child technically doesn't have a body type, well, according to society, but that's a damn lie. It's a lot of fat ass, young kids walking around here, and my baby was not about to be one of them.

"Imani, make sure you don't wear white, because you'll get dirty quick and it'll show, and do not wear a dress or skirt." I said as I stood in her doorway.

"OK mommy." She responded smiling, as she went back into her closet.

It seemed like that was the only time we got along, when it came clothes and shoes. Closing her door, I headed into my bedroom, where I found Ethan leaning against the headboard in the bed, shirtless, typing on his laptop. I stood there for a minute, admiring how fine his ass was. Ethan may not have been an athlete, but working around them all the time damn sure had its effect on him.

When we had our house built, he made sure to add his in-home gym as well. Everything was custom made, and he had all the workout equipment that you could think of in there. Whenever he was home, he made sure to use it faithfully; and it showed.

I worked out in there as well, but most of the time, I just went and got my shit tucked and sucked out of me.

"Why are you staring at me like that?" I heard Ethan ask.

"I was just wondering when you were going to start getting dressed, company will be arriving soon." I said as I walked over to the walk-in closet, and began to undress.

I will, soon as I finish typing up these updated contracts.

"Why are you typing up new contracts, something wrong?" I questioned as I came back out of the closet naked.

Ethan looked up, and his eyes widened as he saw me standing there. It's been a while since we fucked, but I wasn't complaining, because I had Jerome to tie me over. But the way Ethan was staring at me right now, I already knew his ass wanted to piece of this pussy.

"Uh, I figured since the firm keeps getting more clients by the day, I needed to switch up the contracts and revise them, that's all." He explained, still not able to stop staring at me.

I admit, it felt good to be getting this type of attention from my husband right now.

"Why don't you jump in the shower with me." I suggested.

I walked inside the bathroom, and cut the shower on. I put my hair up in a high bun, and got inside. Satisfied that the water temperature was to my liking, I stood underneath the shower head, closed my eyes, and let it beat down on my body. Seconds later, I heard the shower door being pulled opened. My eyes were still closed, but I felt the presence of Ethan tall frame over towering my body.

"Hmm." I moaned out as I felt him washing my back with my loofa.

It felt so good when Ethan was caressing my body, as the body wash traced down to the crack of my ass. he stopped washing my back, and began to massage both of my ass cheeks. Feeling his touch, caused shock waved throughout my body. Ethan and I have always had sexual chemistry between the both of us. Not able to take it anymore, I turned around, and pushed him up against the wall.

Dropping to my knees, I started massaging his already hard dick, in my hands. Then, I took him whole in my mouth. Ethan let out a moan as he leaned his head back against the wall. I began to slow stroke his dick, as I continued to suck him deep. I took one of my hands, and started massaging his balls, which drove him crazy. I continued to suck his dick until he couldn't take it anymore.

"Nah, I wanna come in this pussy." Ethan breathed out loud.

Ethan stood me up by my shoulders, and switched positions with me, by turning me face first towards the wall. Next thing I felt, was his thick dick sliding up in me.

"Aah" I moaned out as he started stroked in and out of me.

Ethan grabbed both of my hands, and pinned them on the wall, as he fucked me hard. All you could hear was the smacking of our bodies against one another. Ethan sucked on my neck from behind, while still fucking the shit out of me.

"Damn, this pussy stay good." Ethan whispered in my ear.

I couldn't even respond back, because the dick was too good to even talk! We fucked in the shower, until the water started to become cold. Finally, Ethan came up in my pussy, and I followed right behind him.

"Now we gotta take this cold ass shower." Ethan joked as we stood in the shower, washing ourselves off.

After we were both done in the bathroom, we started getting ready for the cookout. Since it was hot outside, I decided on wearing a red, low-cut, fitted Michael Kors maxi dress, that displayed all my curves and fat ass, no panties, and some gold Michael Kors sandals to match. Since I had curly textured hair, I was giving it break from my regular sew-in's, and was wearing it loosely in its natural state since it was already wet from the shower. The only make up I put on, was my nude-sheer MAC lipstick. I refused to be sweating like a clown with heavy make-up on in this heat.

Once I was dressed, I looked over at Ethan, and smiled. He was comfortable and sexy in a pair of red Jordan Basketball shorts, a black and red Jordan shirt, and a pair the latest all black Jordan's on his feet.

"I see you trying to match my fly." I said, referring to both of us wearing red.

"You know we have to stay looking good together." He said as he kissed me on my lips. "I'm about to head downstairs, and get prepared for our guest." Ethan announced as he smacked me on my ass, and left out of our bedroom.

I was still standing there, thinking about what Ethan had just said to me, about us having to look good together. Is that what he thought of us now?

CHAPTER 12

Kennedi

It's been a week since Darnell popped up at my apartment, and since then, I haven't heard anything from him. I found that odd since he basically hunted me down, and threatened me, but I wasn't complaining. Hopefully, he finally got it through his thick ass skull that it was over, even know I know that's easier said than done. More than likely, he's probably off fucking with some new bitches he's dealing with, and not paying my ass any attention; at least for the moment. Once the fun wears off, as always, he'll be back to sniffing in my ass like always. Although I used to love when he sweated me and begged me to speak to him, I'm hoping that whoever the chick is that's keeping him occupied, keeps him busy enough so that he can leave me the hell alone.

Making my way into the kitchen, I grabbed me a bottle of water from the fridge and placed it on the counter. Now inside of the pantry, I reached to pick up my family sized bag of Cheddar & Sour Cream Ruffles, a jar of French onion dip, and a small package of cookies. With all of my snacks in hand, I picked up the water, and head into the living room. Taking a seat on the couch, I spread my goodies on the coffee table and powerd on the television. It's Sunday, and

I've been waiting all week to watch all of the movies that are showing today on LMN; which is the Lifetime Movie Network. This week's theme is, Love Gone Wrong, and from the previews, I know I'm in for a treat.

After opening my chips and dip, I prepare to kick back and enjoy my first movie. Picking up the remote, I change the channel and place it beside me. Just as the movie is about to start, my phone rings. Grabbing the remote again, I hit pause and glance down at my phone. Seeing that it's a number that I'm not familiar with, I tap ignore. Since I don't do business on Sunday's, I know that it's not a client. Anyone else can leave a message. Just as I get ready to go back to the movie, the ringing begins yet again. Once more, I tap ignore, only for it start right back up. Blowing a bunch of forced air from my mouth; I snatch up my phone because it's obvious that someone really wants something to keep calling me back to back. With an annoyed look on my face, I slid the button across the screen and answer it.

"This is Kennedi."

"Damn, baby. How many times a nigga gotta call you before you answer?" Darnell asked.

"Mook?" I questioned, even know I'd know his voice anywhere.

"Yeah! Who the hell else would be calling you and calling

you baby?"

I sighed and rolled my eyes. "What do you want, boy?"

"I need you to come pick me up."

"Pick you up?" I turned my nose up. "Where the hell is your car?"

"It's in the impound lot. The day I left your apartment, I got pulled over by the police and they towed my shit," he explained.

"Why would they tow your car?" I asked, and as soon as the words left my lips, I regretted it. I didn't want his ass to think that I actually cared about his car being towed. Truthfully, I was really trying to figure out why the hell he was calling me of all people.

"Man, some dumb shit," he groaned. "I was fucking around in Tatemville, and got a loud music ticket."

"They towed your car for a loud music ticket?" I inquired knowing there was more to the story. With Darnell, there's always more.

"Yeah, well not only because of the music. When they came, me and a few of my niggas were sitting in my car smoking a blunt. So, on top of the loud music ticket, I also got a weed ticket, and then turned around and got arrested because one of those little niggas had some shit on them and didn't cop to it, so we all went down."

Popping a cookie into my mouth, I asked, "What kind of shit?"

"It wasn't nothing major, just a few rocks," he answered in a nonchalant ass tone.

"That's a damn shame."

"Yeah, I know. Since I missed my court date, they put a warrant out for my arrest. Honestly, I forgot all about the shit, until the cop pulled me over. It was like a month or so when it happened, so it slipped my mind. Anyways, not only did he get my car towed, but he locked me up. With nobody to come and pay my bond I had to sit in that bitch for a fucking week," he said. I shook my head because Darnell was always doing some dumb shit.

You see, this is the type of shit that I've been warning him about for years, but of course he never listened to shit people tried to tell him because he thinks he knows it all. Tatemville is this rough neighborhood in Chatham county. It's not super far from where he lives, but it's also not real close either. I'd say about a forty-five-minute drive, and from experience Darnell doesn't mind doing it at least a few times a week.

Darnell can't seem to stay the hell away from that place. At first, I thought it was because he was fucking with some bitch down there, but I've come to find out that it's not just some bitch, it was quite a few bitches. There are a bunch of low-income, project, ghetto and ratchet chicks that live in that area, and from my understanding; Darnell loved to deal with them. I can't even honestly tell you how many times I've heard rumors that he was dealing with another one of those hoes but I know it's a lot. As a matter of fact, the last chick that I caught him with was from Tatemville. The one that he swore up and down that he wasn't messing with, and the same one that he "claims" is only saying that they were because she doesn't like me.

For some reason, Darnell thinks I'm a fool, but I'm not. Even after I caught them coming out of the movie theater together, he still insisted that nothing was going on between the two of them, but I knew better, which is why I decided to call it quits. I figured if ghetto trash was what he wanted, he would never change for me; no matter how hard I tried to get him to. So yeah, he loves Tatemville, and I honestly can't even tell you why. Other than the hoes being downright trashy, the place is hood and dangerous as hell. Darnell has been shot at quite a few times while hanging with his so-called friends, and yet he still can't see that that place means him no good. So, you see, even after everything that has transpired in that place, his dumb ass still hasn't learned his lesson, and now because of that, he may be facing a drug charge.

"You are truly stupid," I mumble.

"Come on, Kennedi. I ain't trying to hear your mouth right now," Darnell groaned. "Can you just come pick me up? I need a fuckin' ride home."

"What?" I asked as I sat up straight on the couch. "Why the hell do you need me to pick you up? Where the fuck are the people you were with who got your ass thrown in there?"

"I don't know where them nigga's at, man. I've been trying to get in contact with 'em since the day I got arrested, but I haven't been able to," he replied and my mouth dropped open. "I'm out here stranded."

"So, you mean to tell me that the muthafucka's who are responsible for you being put in jail haven't answered *any* of your calls?" I paused. "So basically they don't give a fuck about you just like I've been telling your hardheaded ass since you started taking your retarded ass around there!"

"Kennedi, don't start that shit because I don't have time for it. Just come and—" he started but I stopped him before he could finish his sentence.

"No, don't tell me what the fuck to start, because you called me!" I yelled before I started to laugh out of the blue. This shit was truly funny, and Darnell was about to find out that he had me fucked up. "You are a piece of work, Mook. You always make sure to call me when shit is down for you, but those are the same muthafucka's that you chose to give all your time to. I told they weren't shit but you wouldn't listen, and now look at your dumb ass." I shook my head. "I don't know what you're going to do, and truthfully I don't care. What I would suggest is that you call ya boys again and see if they'll finally answer. Better yet, dial up one of those bitches you can't seem to stay away from and have them come get you. If they can find a ride… or Uber. At the end of the day, it's your choice, but I can't do nothing for you," I told him before I pulled the phone away from my ear.

I could hear him yelling something as I hung up, but of course, I couldn't make out what it was, nor did I care. At this point, I was done with it. When my phone immediately started to ring again, I tapped ignore, place it into do not disturb mode and sat it face down on the coffee table. I wasn't about to play games with Darnell's dumb ass today. It was his own fault that he was in the situation he was in, so there was no way in hell that I was going to go rescue him. That was one of the reasons why he stays fucking up because every time he get's his retarded ass into something he can't get out of, either me, or his father runs to his rescue. I'm done, and apparently, his dad is too because if not, he would have gone and got him, and Darnell wouldn't have had to call me. Either way, oh well. That's no longer my problem.

Now annoyed, I pick back up my remote, and press play. As the opening of the movie starts, my eyes are on the screen, but my mind isn't really paying attention. Snatching my phone up from the table, I flip it over and look at it, only to see that Darnell has called me five more times. After clearing my notifications from his annoying ass, I go to my messages and search for my best friend's name. I need to talk to her right now because my emotions are all over the place, and other than my parents, she's the only one who can get my mind right.

ME: *What's up, Snicker Doodle?*

BESTIE: *Nothing much, Pookie. Just catching up on some studying.*

ME: *You're always studying. I miss you. (sad emoji)*

My best friend was over three hundred miles away at North Carolina A&T, and I missed her dearly. So much so, that I sometimes wished that I could turn back the hands of time to when we were kids.

Tasha and I had been best friends since we were in kindergarten. It was the very first day of school, and apparently, we both were scared of leaving our parents are ending up being sat beside one another to be each others company. Not sure what happened, because I can't remember that far, but since then we've been as thick as thieves. We literally did everything together. So much so, that our parents even got close. They had no choice with their daughters being as close as we were. We made sure to see each other daily at school and out, and we even did the whole sleepover thing every weekend; whether it was at my house or at hers. That tells you just how close we were. Our parents used to call us Frick and Frack, and we didn't care one bit.

Back then when we used to talk about being older, we never once thought that we would be apart. I guess as children you don't think about stuff like that. You think about the right now, and always believe that your best friend will always be around. We used to talk about growing up, getting our very first apartment together, and doing pretty much everything side by side. Things like having big, extravagant weddings where we'd marry handsome brothers, and having twins at the same time. We'd move into these big houses with the white picket fences and the dog, with the pool in the back. Everything was all planned out; at least in our minds, it was. You know how that goes. It's kid stuff, and things like that rarely come true. Never once did we think about college, or the "real life" stuff.

I remember it was our senior year in high school. Tasha and I were at her house. It was the weekend, and we were sitting on her bed, while she anxiously started to open the many envelopes that she'd received from all of the colleges that she'd applied for. One by one she read off acceptance letters. I sat there genuinely proud of my best friend and all of her accomplishments. She had worked hard to get into those schools, and she deserved it. Since I had already decided that I was going to take a year or two off before I started college, I silently hoped that Tasha would go somewhere close. My heart broke when she jumped off the bed and screamed. In her hand she held the acceptance letter from North Carolina. That shit broke my heart. Like I said before, I was extremely proud of my friend, but the selfish side of me wanted her to stay right here in Savannah by my side.

BESTIE: *Awww, Pook, I miss you too. I'll be back in less than a month on break.*

ME: *Yes! I can't wait. Hopefully, it'll right on time for mom and dad's anniversary party. I was actually thinking about coming up there to see you before that. I really need to get away.*

BESTIE: *Oh yeah, that's right. Year 25. I've got to think of something nice to get them. You know you're more than welcome to come up anytime. I have finals coming up, so I have to make time to study. All other time will be dedicated to you. Now, what's going on, and who's ass do I need to kick?*

I laughed at how fast she was ready to go to war when it came to me. Tasha was a firecracker, and she didn't play about her bestie. There had been plenty of times when she's had to go off on Darnell's ass for the way that he'd treated me. I remember once they almost came to blows because she caught him at the gas station with another bitch in his car. I'm still surprised that they didn't because from what I was told, Tasha ran up on his and started to beat his ass as if he were a nigga off the street. Can't lie, I was happy as hell because Darnell's dog ass deserved it and made me wish that I could've been there to see it. It's probably for the best, because I know me and know that between the two of us Darnell would've been fucked up; his little bitch too.

I spent the next thirty minutes texting Tasha before we promised to speak later. Just as I finished up a conversation with her, I saw that I had a text from Ethan. I rolled my eyes as I read the message.

ETHAN: *Hey beautiful*

Still looking down at my phone, I didn't even bother to respond. Right now as annoyed as I am with him, it's probably better that I don't say anything in return. It had been days since we'd spoken. Every time I call him, he doesn't answer, only texting me back to let me know that he's busy and will call me later. When later rolls around that call never came. It's like he just forgot about me altogether. Apparently, I'm not important anymore. It had gotten so bad that I've haven't reached out to Ethan in the last three days because I'm tired of getting the cold shoulder. In those three days he hasn't bothered to call me once; only sending this weak ass text. We went from talking on the phone a few times a day, to nothing but texts, and even those are far and few in between. I'm not sure what has gotten into him, but I'm not feeling it.

With that being said, right now my attitude for the moment is, fuck Ethan. He can keep his texts, and broken phone call promises because I'm done with the entire thing. My intuition is telling me that shit ain't right, and it's usually never wrong. For all I know he's probably laid up with his baby momma, and if that's the case, she can keep his ass. I'm not chasing a man who clearly is all of a sudden too busy to have a simple conversation. I can't front, my feelings are a bit hurt, but I'll be alright. If Ethan wants me, he's going to have to prove it, because until then, I'm going to be the one who is too busy and I'm not longer thinking about his ass. Picking up my remote control, I play my movie again. This time my mind is clear and it has all of my attention.

CHAPTER 13

Chace

It's been a week since we had the fourth of July cookout at our house, and Ethan and I have been on good terms. He's been more attentive, and coming home at a decent hour of the night. We even had been having family dinners together, which Imani loved. Although I enjoyed this side of Ethan, I knew that he was only *temporarily* acting right, only because I had confronted him about that bitch Kennedi; who I have yet to get more information on, but in due time I will. So, I knew all of this that he was doing, was temporary. Then, when Ethan thought that he had done just enough to shut my fucking mouth, his ass would be right back to doing him.

That's why I was still kicking it Jerome. When Ethan would leave for work in the mornings, I was sliding my ass over to Jerome spot, and getting dicked down. Speaking of Jerome, he showed up at the cookout, as a guest of my brothers of course, and we snuck off for a quickie in Ethan home gym. Ethan was so damn drunk, and surprisingly having a good time with my folks, that his ass hadn't even noticed that I was missing for those thirty minutes or so.

I was shocked that Jerome had even showed up, because I didn't even invite him, but, I played it cool, and welcomed him like I did everyone else. All throughout that day, he kept eyeing me, and watching how my ass was moving like jelly every time I moved. Jerome would even look pissed whenever Ethan would playfully slap me on the ass, or give me occasional kisses. I was praying no one else would notice how much Jerome was paying attention to us, but that shit turned me on to see how jealous he was acting.

Finally, Jerome sent a text to my phone, and asked me to meet him in my downstairs foyer. Since everyone was out in the backyard, occupied, I replied telling him okay, but we had to make it quick. When I went inside, Jerome was already waiting by the foyer, texting on his phone.

"What's up?" I whispered to him, as I looked around to make sure no one was watching us.

"We need to duck off somewhere real quick." Jerome said.

"How the fuck are we supposed to do that, with a house full of people Jerome?"

"Shit, that's not my problem. All I know, is that I need to feel that pussy since you wanna keep walking your ass around here in that sexy ass dress with no panties on." he smirked.

"How do you know I don't have any panties on?" I questioned, still looking around.

"Because I know you, that's how. Now, where can we go?"

Standing there for a few seconds, I was contemplating on where Jerome and I could sneak off to. Then, it dawned on me.

"Follow me." I instructed, walking in front of him.

Jerome followed behind me, as I led him down to the basement, to Ethan home gym. I went down first, and told Jerome to lock the door when he came behind me.

"Damn, ya'll really loaded. This look like some Planet Fitness type of shit." Jerome said as he looked around.

Walking over to one the benches, I sat down on it, and cocked my legs open.

"You gone keep paying attention to the equipment, or are you gonna bring that equipment you got between your legs and come handle this?" I flirted.

Jerome looked over at me, and licked his lips. I started playing with my pussy, with sliding my two index fingers in and out of me. I know I had just had sex earlier with my husband, but this sneaking shit Jerome and I were doing right now, turned me the fuck on. Jerome walked over to where I was, and kneeled at the foot of the bench where I was sitting.

Grabbing me by my thighs, he pulled me closer to him, and dove head first in between my honey pot.

"Hmm" I moaned out as his tongue played ping-pong with clit.

I thrusted my hips back and forth, fucking Jerome mouth.

"I'm about to cum baby." I whispered to him out loud.

Right when I said that, Jerome hopped up, pulled down his shorts, and plunged his thick dick inside me.

"Yes!" I hollered out a little too loud.

Wrapping my arms around his neck, Jerome fucked the dog shit out of me. We each covered one another mouth, reframing us from making noises out loud, but you could still hear the smacking sounds of our bodies. Not being able to hold back anymore, I exploded. Shortly after, Jerome came all up inside of me as well. We both got up, and went inside of the bathroom Ethan had down there also, and did a quick wash off.

Once we were done, I headed upstairs first, just to make sure the coast was clear. Soon as I saw that it was, I whispered down for Jerome to come up. We both walked back out into the cookout, separately of course, and continued the rest of the day as if nothing happened. After everyone had finally left that night, I helped Ethan drunk ass upstairs, where he fell asleep in our bed, still fully clothed. I made sure Imani showered, and went to bed, and then I did the same.

"Chace, did you hear me?" I looked up to see Ethan standing in front of me, holding Imani's hand.

I was so caught up in thinking about what happened on the fourth of July, that I didn't even see nor hear Ethan when he came into the living room.

"I'm sorry baby, I was thinking about something Tricia had told me earlier, what did you say?" I asked looking up at Ethan.

"I said, that I'm about to take Imani to the mall, to Build A Bear. She had been asking me for some time now, and since I have the day off, I figured I'd use it and take her. You wanna come with us?" Ethan offered.

Now, normally, I would jump at the chance to hit up the mall, and burn up the stores, but sitting here thinking about Jerome, caused my pussy to yearn for him.

"No, that's okay baby. You two can have a father-daughter day. I'll just probably go hang out at Tricia house until you two get back." I lied.

"Humph, Tricia house." Ethan snorted.

"What's that supposed to mean?" I asked, sitting up on the couch.

"You know how I feel about you hanging with Tricia ghetto, hood rat ass. That chick stay in some shit, and I don't want my wife caught up in none of her antics." Ethan ranted.

It was no secret that Ethan didn't like Tricia. Just like everyone else, he had heard the stories about her and how she got down. But, as much as my husband didn't want me being around her, I had too; Tricia was my all-time alibi.

"Ethan, like I have told you plenty of times before this; whatever Tricia do, is her business. It has nothing to do with me. Just have fun with your daughter, and I'll see you two when you get home." I reached up, and kissed him lightly on his lips.

I refused to fuck up my time I was about to spend with Jerome, by standing here and arguing with Ethan; especially over that bitch Tricia. Shortly after him and Imani left out the door, and I called Jerome.

"Yeah" he answered the phone on the third ring.

"I need to see you." I spoke, getting right to the point.

"Damn girl, I just gave you some of this good dick two days ago." Jerome laughed into the phone.

From the noise in the background, I could tell he was out and about. His ass was probably trying to front in front of those tired ass niggas he usually hung out with.

"Whatever Jerome, are you going to meet me at the spot or not?"

"Yeah, I'll be there in an hour; but I can't stay long because I got some shit to handle." Jerome told me.

I hung up the phone without saying anything else, and got up to head upstairs to take a quick shower. Jerome thought his ass was just gonna fuck me and leave in a hurry, but he had another thing coming. I pulled up to the spot about fifteen minutes before Jerome was scheduled to get here, and let myself inside. Putting my purse down on the table, I took my shoes off, and untied my coat. Underneath, I had nothing on but a pair of thongs and bra.

Walking over to the liquor bar, I pulled out the Patron, and poured me a shot. Going back over to my purse, I pulled out my already rolled-up blunt, and lit that shit. Getting comfortable on the bed, I laid there with my drink in one hand, and my blunt in the other. Finally, Jerome walked his fine ass through the door. The way he had his pants half way sagging off his ass, showing the top of his briefs, wife beater showing off his triceps, and fitted cap, caused my pussy to pulsate.

Jerome had that thug swag about him, and I liked that shit. I felt like I had the best of both worlds when it came to him and Ethan. Ethan was the more corporate, stable, take-home to your momma type. The man you become a wife too, and never have to worry about going broke or hungry with. Jerome, on the other hand, was a street dude, who got money however he could, and you had to keep his ass in the background type of dude. Whichever one I was in the mood for at the time, was who I dealt with.

"I see you already waiting on a nigga." Jerome said to me as he put his keys on the table next to my purse.

"I told yo ass over the phone, that I wanted you. So, I didn't wanna waste any time when I got here." I replied as I placed my glass and smoke on the side table, and stood up on my knees on the bed.

Jerome walked over to the bed, and pushed me back roughly, so that I was lying flat on my back. He pulled his shirt over his head, unbuckled his jeans, and pulled them down. Right when he was about to climb on top of me, we heard a loud banging on the door.

"Who the fuck is that?" I sat up alarmed.

"I don't fucking know, but it better not be your husband." Jerome replied as he stood up, and pulled his pants back up.

Whoever it was, banged on the door again.

"Jerome, I know yo' ass is up in there with that bitch!" I heard a woman yell out.

I did sigh a slight relief when I realized that it wasn't Ethan at the door, but then, I became annoyed that it was one of Jerome's jump offs. The bitch continued to bang on the door, and curse us out while standing out there.

"Jerome, you need to handle that shit before someone calls the police." I warned him as I leaned back against the head board.

"Fuck man!" Jerome hollered out as he snatched the door open.

"Asia what-"

"Move the fuck outta my way Jerome!" The chick cut him off and barged into the room.

"So, this is why the fuck you ran off, to come lay-up with this old ass bitch!" She screamed out, pointing at me.

I chuckled as I stood up, preferably to give this bad body, sponge bob shaped bitch, a view of this *old bitch* body. The way she turned her nose up at me, and rolled her eyes, caused me to laugh even harder out loud.

"Oh you think this shit is funny hoe?" She said as she moved towards me.

"Actually, I do. And I suggest you tone it down, because I won't be too many of those names you keep calling me." I for-warned her ass.

One thing about me, if I had to get my hands dirty and fuck a bitch up, then I would.

"Bitch-" Before she could say anything else, I punched that hoe dead in her mouth. She stumbled back, and fell against the wall, hitting her head. I ran over to her, and tried to beat her ass some more, but Jerome stopped me, and lifted me up in midair.

"Aye man, chill out." Jerome said to me.

"Whatever, just get this bitch out of here, so that we can finish what we started." I replied snatching away out of his arms.

I walked back over to the night table, breathing heavy. I grabbed my blunt, and lit it back up. Taking a pull from it, I held it in a little longer than normal, then blew the smoke out.

Asia, or whatever the hoe name is, slowly stood up, holding the back of her head.

"After all the shit I have done for you Jerome. The hiding your drugs, putting money on your books every time you get locked up, sneaking weed in the jail through my pussy, you still wanna keep being out here trying me with random bitches! I'm so done with yo ass!" She cried out as she stood straight up, and headed towards the door to leave.

"Asia, just go home and I'll be by there later." Jerome tried to reason with her.

"Nah nigga, fuck you!" Asia screamed as she held the door open.

"Girl, either take your ass out the door, or come back in here and join us." I said to her, grinning.

Asia stood there with her mouth wide open, shocked at what I had just said to her. There was no way in hell I was letting that nasty looking bitch touch me, but if she wanted to suck Jerome dick, then so be it. Asia shook her head as the tears fell from her eyes.

"You two nasty muthafuckas deserve one another." With that said, she left out the room, and slammed the door.

Looking over at Jerome, I put the blunt back down in the ashtray, and laid back down on the bed.

"Now, can we finish this please?"

CHAPTER 14

Kennedi

Ding Dong

Climbing out of the bathtub, I wrapped my towel tightly around my body, before placing my terrycloth robe over my shoulders and tying it closed. Once my still wet feet are slid into my house slippers, I opened the bathroom door and dart down the hall. It was still very early in the morning, and I was trying to enjoy a nice relaxing bath, but unfortunately, someone else had other things in mind. As I made my way through the house and towards the front door, I snatched the hair bonnet off of my head and stuffed it into the robe pocket. Shaking my head, I allow my locks to fall free and down my back. Can't be walking to the door looking any old kind of way, because you never know who could be on the other side. Now at the door, I stand on my tippy toes and glance out of the small glass window. When I do I see that it's a young looking guy on the other side.

"Who is it?" I asked still looking out of the glass.

"Express florist," he responded. "I have a delivery for Kennedi Carter."

"Hold on a second," I told him before I adjusted my robe to make sure that I was completely covered. Once I was satisfied that I was, I undid the latch and opened the door.

"Good morning, Ma'am. Are you by chance Kennedi Carter?"

"I am," I answered as I reached out and accepted the brightly colored flowers from his hands. After signing that I'd received them, the guy thanked me, before he headed back down my stairs to his truck.

With my flowers in hand, I closed my door, walked over to my living area and placed the footed flared vase on top of the coffee table. Taking a seat on the sofa, I smile as I take a closer look at my delivery. The vase is clear but lined with some kind of tropical leaves that start at the bottom, and slightly spill out of the top. The bouquet itself consisted of a mix of blue hydrangea's, lavender roses, and orchids in both green and violet. There are a few small, pieces of lily grass inside, which brings the entire thing together perfectly. Leaning in, I took a whiff and I realize that not only are the flowers gorgeous, but they smell amazing as well. Finally, I remove the card from the holder and open it up. There's a small note inside that reads:

Kennedi,

Please accept these flowers as a start of me letting you know just how sorry I am for these last few weeks. I feel so guilty for being as busy as I've been which caused me to neglect you. I want you to know that it was not intentional and that I would never purposely do anything to jeopardize what we have. Please forgive me because I am truly sorry. If it's okay, I would like to call you today. Can you please answer, because I really would love to hear your voice. I'd be lying if I said that I didn't miss the hell out of you right now, so please answer. Again, I'm sorry, and I hope to be able to talk to you later.

Ethan

Placing the note on the top of the table, I can't help but smile as I leaned back against the couch. Although I'm still upset with Ethan, the flowers were a nice touch. They at least let me know that I'm on his mind because lately I've been thinking otherwise. After reading the message about him being sorry, and missing me, I guess I'll finally go ahead and answer his call this time. Lately, I've been ignoring both those, as well as the text messages. I figured if he was too busy to speak to me; I'll make myself unavailable as well. I wasn't playing when I said that I wasn't dealing with him, and that his ex-wife, or whoever the hell else can have him. Not sure who Ethan is used to dealing with, but I don't

tolerate feeling as if I'm being ignored, and I'll be damn if I chase a man; no matter
how successful he is.

To be honest, even though I missed talking to him as well, I was willing to just walk away. Hell, it's not like I have a whole lot invested into this relationship. These few weeks gave me a glimpse into the reality of how things would be if things got serious, and I don't like it one bit. I can't imagine not being able to reach my man who is in an entirely different state. Add in the fact that his ex-wife, who is also the mother of his only child, is in that very state as well. Oh no, that shit ain't gone fly. Whenever Ethan and I speak, I'm definitely going to let him know my feelings, and let him know that flowers aren't just going to fix things. If he can't understand my frustrations and try to work something out, then we should just go ahead and call it quits while it's still early. With my mind still on my expected phone call later, I take one last look at the flowers, before I stand up from the couch and head back to finish my bath.

Thirty minutes later, I'm feeling not only refreshed, but relaxed as well. With a towel wrapped around my still damp body, I made my way over to the bathroom sink and turned on the water. After I've handled my morning hygiene, I head into my room to get dressed. Since I don't have any plans to go anywhere today, I put on nothing but a long t-shirt and underwear. I was in the process of going into my office, when I realized that I forgot something. Going back into the bathroom, I pull out the top drawer, and grab my birth control pill case. After filling up the glass that I keep on the counter, I open up the container and see that I only have three pills left.

"Shit," I whispered, finally remembering that I was supposed to call in my refill a few days ago. As I threw my head back and swallowed the tiny pill, I made a mental note to call the pharmacy once I made it into my office.

Entering the bedroom that I'd transformed into my personal office, I realize that it's times like this that I appreciate being my own boss. It's nothing like handling business while dressed in pretty much anything you want. Not that I mind putting on professional attire, because I'll do it without hesitation, but it's also nice to kick back and relax sometimes. Taking a seat at my computer, I power it on and immediately pull up my email to see what's new. When I noticed that I've receive not only payment for my services, but also confirmation of my flight to California as well, I can't help but to do a little dance in my seat. I'm stoked, because I've been on pins and needles as I waited on this new client to come through. I knew that that if I was able to get them in the bag, things would be lovely for me, and after looking at my payment that posted into my bank account; I was right.

"That's what the hell I'm talking about!" I yell excitedly.

My mini celebration is interrupted by the ringing of my phone from my bedroom. Jumping up, I rushing in there to grab it. With the confirmation and payment just posted, it might be my client, and I don't want to miss her call. Inside my room, I pick up my phone and see that once again Darnell is calling. I don't know how many times I will have to tell his slow ass to lose my damn number until he understands. The shit is annoying, and makes me really want to change my shit. The only thing that's stopping me is the fact that it's tied to my business account, and getting a new number would really be a hassle. Pressing ignore, I take my phone back with me to my office to finish going through my emails. Almost immediately it starts to ring again. This time, it's from an unknown number. At first I don't plan on answering it, but figure that it maybe a new client calling for a consultation, so I go for it.

"This is Kennedi," I answer as I take a seat in my computer chair.

"I like how you can answer this number, but you can't pick up when you see that it's me calling!" Darnell barked.

"Dude," I sighed, "You gotta be kidding me right now. Whose phone are you calling me from?"

"Don't worry about it. You at home?"

"Why?"

"Because I'm about to come over. I—"

"No the fuck you ain't!" I yelled. I don't know what the fuck he thought, but that shit is not about to happen.

"Man, kill all that noise. I need to talk to you about something," he spoke.

"Mook, you already know that me and you ain't got shit to talk about," I tell him while I type out a message to my client thanking her for the payment, and letting her know that I'll see her in a few days.

"See, I'm trying to be nice, but you keep playing with me."

I pull my phone away from my ear and just stare at it for a moment. Darnell has gotten on my last nerve, and I'm sick of his shit. I'm not sure why he thinks that I'm just supposed to do whatever it is that he says, but I think it's time that I nip this shit here in the bud right now. If not, he's going to keep talking to me crazy, and expecting shit that he no longer deserves from me. What we had is dead, and even if he doesn't want to hear it, he's going to have to accept it. He's about to see a side of me that he hasn't seen in a while.

"Listen, this shit stops now!" I yelled. "I don't know why you keep acting like what I'm saying is new to you when I've been saying this same shit for weeks! We don't have *nothing* to talk about anymore, do you hear me?" I asked, even though I wasn't expecting an answer. "I'm done! It's over and I'm

moving on, and it's all because of your fuck up, not mine!"

"I keep telling you—" Darnell started, but I interjected real quick.

"You see, that's the thing," I scoffed. "You don't have to tell me shit when I've seen it with my own two eyes. I'm not stupid over you anymore, Mook, and it's time that you let the shit that we had go because I'm sick of you barking out orders like you run shit this way, when you don't. Stop trying to pop up at my house, stop telling me what I'm going to and what I'm not going to do, stop the threats and please stop calling my damn phone," I said damn near out of breath. I was tired of being nice. This nigga had me fucked up.

"Man, whatever. You can talk all the shit you want, but it ain't over. I don't believe it for one second," Darnell argued. "You say this shit every time, so I ain't trying to hear it."

All I could do was laugh at his stupid ass, because even after everything I'd just said, he was still on the same dumb shit. It was like it all went in one ear and came out the other.

"You know what… fuck it, because it doesn't even matter," I laughed. "You're stupid. Always have been, and apparently you always will be. Just stop calling my phone, and stay the fuck away from me withcho stupid ass!"

"Bitch, you better watch who you calling stupid!" he roared. "Don't make me come over there and—"

"And do what, Mook?" I asked. "You ain't no killer, so please stop pretending like you're one. Don't let the fact that you hang with nigga's who are about that life fool you into thinking that you are too. That shit doesn't scare me. Oh, and watch your mouth when you speak to me, or at least put a handle on that shit and call me Ms. Bitch. I'm not one of these little whores that you deal with, so you better fucking act like you know."

"See, I guess I'm just going to have to show you how I get down. Smack you in your fucking mouth a few times."

"Muthafucka, I wish the fuck you would!" I challenged him. "You got me fucked up if you believe for one second that I'm just going to allow you to hit me. Try that shit and watch how fast shit will get real for your dumb ass!"

"Hoe please. I ain't even worried. You letting that little funky ass job go to your head and you think you can talk to me crazy. Let's not forget, *bitch*, that you were broke not too long ago, so quit letting that social media hype go to your head," Darnell laughed. "Keep talking reckless if you want to though, because I'm gonna see you," he told me before he hung up the phone in my ear.

I sat there for a minute with my mouth opened. I couldn't believe that he went there, knowing damn well that it was all a lie. First and foremost, he has never been one to hurt a fly. Not calling him soft, but he damn sure wasn't no killer. Those niggas that he hangs with in Tatemville do the dirty work. Darnell is just their designated driver. They fuck with him because he pays for shit, and carts them around the city because he is the only one who has a license. Second, I have never been broke. Even when I wasn't working and was in school, I was well taking care of. My father made sure of that. My dad has worked hard all of my life to provide for my mother and I, and even though we aren't Bill Gates rich, we've always been a part of the upper class, so Darnell can stop it with those lies, because he knew better.

I push him and all of the stupid ass drama that he brought to the back of my head and got back to work. As much as I doubt it, I really do hope that he doesn't do anything stupid, because if so, I will do anything in my power to make sure that his dumb ass won't fuck with me again, and you can bet the bank on that.

*****

"I'm not lying. I've missed you something terrible," Ethan swore. It was a little after four o'clock in the afternoon and he had just gotten off of work.

"Humph, you could've fooled the hell outta me," I told him as I rolled my eyes. Like I said, I loved the flowers, but he wasn't getting back in my good graces that easy. "Made me feel like you didn't want to be bothered, so I said fuck it."

"It was not like that, I promise. I was just caught up with these new clients I just picked up, and wasn't able to talk as much as I would have liked."

"I hear you." Lying on my back in bed, I looked up at the ceiling. Although I still feel some kind of way, it felt good to talk to Ethan again. I guess I kind of missed him too. "I don't believe the shit though."

"Come on, Kennedi, give me a break."

"I will not," I snapped. "You tell me all these sweet things, and ignore the hell out of me for days at a time. Now that you're free to talk or whatever, now you think that I'm just supposed to be cool with it? I don't fucking think so. Been there done that, and I'm over it."

"I don't even know what to say right now." I heard him say. A few moments go by without either of us saying anything. I was quiet because I'd said what I felt, so I left it up to him. "You have the right to be mad, but like I said before things just got hectic. Between working and sleeping, I barely had any time for Imani," he sighed. "I'm not saying this as an excuse, but I'm telling you because it's what happened. Look, Kennedi, I really like you and I hope you know that. I love what we have right now and don't want to lose it. So, please tell me what I need to do to make this right"

With my fingers twirling around a stray string from my throw pillow, I thought about what Ethan had just said. Maybe he was extremely busy and didn't have time to speak. Just as soon as that thought entered my mind, the logical side of me kicked it.

"I get all that, Ethan, and I know that things can get chaotic. What I'm saying is that people make time for the things they want. You can't tell me that you didn't take a break *at all* for more than a week. Shit, I get busy at times, but I make sure to reach out to the people I care about. Whether it be during my lunch, while I'm taking a bath, stuck at a stop light or using the damn bathroom… it takes no time to send a simple text," I explained shooting his busy claims down.

"You're right, and I'm sorry I didn't think to do that," he apologized. "Again, what can I do to make this right?"

"I don't know. If you're so busy, maybe you don't have time for this. Maybe we should take a break or something."

"Don't say that," Ethan pleaded. "I'll try harder to make time, I promise."

"I guess, we'll see."

"I'm going to show you. Now that that's out the way, what's been up with you? Fill me in on anything I've missed."

"You first, Mr. M. I. A.," I shot back.

"Hmmm, okay. Well, as I mentioned, I have quite a few new clients. I haven't been able to spend a lot of time with Imani, but I was able to take her to Build-A-Bear yesterday. She loves that place," he told me, and I could hear the smile in his voice as he spoke about his daughter. "Other than that, I've been swamped. Your turn."

"Just like you, I've been working, and I've also gotten another client. I just sealed the deal today."

"Care to share who it is?" Ethan probed.

"Let's just say that I'm going to California to decorate the master bedroom of the house in the Bay Area, and the client is the wife of a recent NBA champion."

"I know you ain't talking about who I think you are."

"If it's the player that's been said to be one of the greats, then yes I am!" I gushed, still excited that I'd actually landed this contract.

"Hell yeah!" Ethan shouted. "I'm happy for you, baby, and I'm really proud of you."

"Thank you." I smiled. "I'm still in shock. This entire thing feels like a dream."

"Well, you deserve it, and so much more," he told me.

"Thank you," I said again.

"Don't thank me, I need to thank you."

Sitting up in the bed, I cock my head to the side. "Thank me for what?" I asked fiddling with the edge of my comforter.

"For coming into my life," he replied. "I know I've been out the way for a while, but I really do care for you, Kennedi, and I'm glad to have someone like you in my life."

"Aww, thank you, Ethan." I blushed.

"I'm serious. You are the perfect catch. You're beautiful, smart, loving, down to earth, and you work hard for your money. I know you always have to get on me about buying you things, but I'm honestly happy that you have your own money," Ethan revealed. "Not to bring her up in the mix or compare you to her, but with Chace I've always been the one to foot the bill. Not saying that I use to mind because I didn't. I'm a man, and I'm supposed to take care of my household. It's just that to know that if some shit goes down, I know that you can help me get us back afloat, whereas she couldn't and wouldn't do that. You got that drive, and won't settle for just enough. Baby, I can tell you want the world and aren't going to sit around and wait for a man to give it to you. You are going to get it yourself."

After hearing Ethan's views of me, I melted. It felt good to have a man tell you that he's fine with you working towards your goals. Darnell never wanted that. He didn't say it right away, but I later found out that he hated my job, and didn't want me to work. The reason being is because he wanted to me have to do depend on him for everything I needed, so it would be harder for me to walk away. Fuck that! I don't think I could ever be the housewife type. While I commend my mother for doing it, and praise my father for allowing her to, that's not me. From the day that I received my very first paycheck from my father, I knew that making my own money was what I wanted to do, and I was going to do that, until I couldn't do it anymore.

"I hate to sound like a broken record, but thank you, Ethan. I really appreciate it."

"No problem. Like I said before, you deserve it," he repeated. "So, when do you have to go to the house?"

"My flight is booked for next Wednesday," I told him. "They won't be there, but they have someone who will let me in."

"Cool. How about I meet you out there and we can spend some time once you're done working your magic?"

"Really?"

"Hell yeah!" he chuckled. "I told you I've missed you."

"Well, I'll be there for almost two weeks. How much time do you have?" I was getting excited at the thought of spending time with him again.

"As much time as you need."

"Shut up!" I laughed. "Are you serious?"

"I am."

"So, you can stay the entire two weeks with me?" I asked for clarification.

"You got it. Just send me your flight information, and I'll see if I could get on the same one. If not, I'll find one not far behind."

"OK, I'll do that now," I said as I picked up my iPad and pulled up my email. After quickly forwarding him my ticket info, I told Ethan, "I just sent it."

"Good. OK, I'm going to handle all that when I get home. I'm also going to book a hotel. I know the client usually provides you one, but that's for you. I'll pay for one for us. Do you know where you'll be staying?"

"Yeah, at the Claremont Club in Berkeley," I told him.

"That's what's up! I don't know about that one, but I stayed at the one in Dallas, and it was real nice, so I know that one won't be much different. It's good to know that they put you up well."

"Yeah, my clients usually take good care of me while I'm working."

"I see," he chuckled. "Well, once I get everything situated, I'll send you over my info, and we can make this happen."

"Sounds good to me," I responded with a bright smile.

"Alright, let me go. I'll call you either later on tonight… I promise."

"OK," I giggled. "I'll talk to you later."

"That you will. Goodnight Kennedi," Ethan said.

"Goodnight," I told him before we disconnected the call.

Dropping my phone beside me, I laid back onto my pillow. With my thoughts on spending time with Ethan in California, my heart started beating a mile a minute. I laughed, because it's crazy that he has that kind of effect on me. I guess that's what smooth words and a handsome face would do to do. Jumping out of my bed, I make my way to the closet to find something to wear. I have a few hours left to hit the mall, and now that I'll be seeing my baby in a few days, I've got some shopping to do. Gotta make sure I'm sexy, because I plan to make up on lost time.

CHAPTER 15

Chace

When I say I know my husband like the back of my damn hand, I knew his ass! Just as I predicted, Ethan went right back to his old ways. I knew all that *good behavior* shit was only temporary, since I caught him trying to be slick with that Kennedi bitch. Once he thought things had calmed down with us, he went right back to bringing his ass home whenever he felt the need too, and being damn sneaky. But little did he know, I had a trick for that ass.

Last week when Ethan came home and claimed that he had to go away to California on business, and would be gone for two weeks, I knew this nigga had done bumped his head! Now, I do know sudden trips do come into play, but for two weeks? Naw, he must have thought that I was really some type of fool. His ass had never spent that much time away from home, so I knew that it was more to it. So, me being the bitch that I am, I started getting on my investigating shit. First, I had to act the norm with Ethan, so that he wouldn't suspect that I knew anything. With that, I did my usual ranting about his ass leaving and being gone that long. Then, I walked around the house with an attitude and not speaking to him, which allowed him to keep doing shit and thinking that he was getting away with it. All the while, I started snooping and trying to find shit out on my own.

Honestly, I would have just let it all go, and chalk this up like I did all of his previous flings, because I know that it would be over soon. But when he announced about being gone for two weeks, I knew this bitch must be different. I didn't give a damn if I was fucking another nigga outside of my marriage, I still didn't want another female having her hooks into my husband. Knowing that Ethan would keep his phone locked and secured to his hip, since I last confronted him, I knew I had to go another route. Picking up my phone, I called Tricia.

"What's up, bitch," she answered the phone.

"Aye, you still fucking with that snake ass cop Jerry?" I asked her.

"Girl hell yeah. You know I love tricking off that nigga," Tricia laughed.

"Good, because I'm about to give you a phone number that I need you to give to him, and have him give you some information on the person it belongs too," I said.

"Ooh bitch, who Ethan fucking around with now?" Tricia asked a little too loud for my taste.

See, this is why I hated like ever telling Tricia about the few times I had caught Ethan fucking around. This bitch also made sure to remind me of the shit every chance she got.

"Look Tricia, just do this for me, and I'll shoot you a quick two hundred," I offered.

"Shit, that's all I needed to hear. Text me the number, and I'll hit Jerry up," she replied.

I hung up the phone without saying anything else to her ass, and text her the number. I ended up getting into Ethan's Sprint account online by putting in Imani's birthday as his password. The nigga was so predictable with that shit. I felt like I had hit the jackpot when it worked and his call logs and text messaging came into view. By him having a lot of clients, I spent damn near and hour going through all of his messages and calls.

One particular number kept sticking out to me. Ethan was calling this number mostly during the day, but the text messages were made more during the night. Reading the messages and comparing the number, I already knew that it had to be Kennedi. The conversations between her and my husband was the type of conversations that he should have been having with me. Ethan was feeling this bitch, and I wasn't about to stand for that.

After reading everything, I placed my phone down next to me and back in my recliner lounger next to the pool in my back yard. It was early Saturday afternoon, and Imani had a few of her friends over swimming. As usual, Ethan wasn't home, so I was laying out back relaxing, sipping on a strawberry daiquiri, and watching the girls. With my shades on, I closed my eyes for a while, and let the sun beat down on my body when I heard my phone ring. I picked it back up, and saw that it was Jerome calling me. Sucking my teeth, I declined the call. I was still pissed at him from the last time we were together, and one of his ghetto bitches showed up and caused a scene. I blamed his ass for not keeping his hood rats in control.

Hearing my phone ring again, I already knew that it was Jerome calling me back.

"What," I finally answered, sounding disinterested.

"Oh, so it's like that now?" Jerome asked.

"Jerome, what the hell you want?" I asked him a low tone, so that Imani's lil grown ass wouldn't hear me.

If she did, her ass would surely run to her daddy and tell him I was talking to another man.

"Why the fuck you talking to me like I'm one of these fuck niggas in the street?" Jerome yelled.

Him raising his voice was not intimating me at all. If he hasn't figured out why I haven't answered his calls or texts these past two weeks, then that shit was on him.

"Well, since you fuck with trash, then maybe you are those type of niggas in the streets," I shot at his ass as I took a sip from my drink.

"Aye, watch yo fucking mouth before I put something in that shit to shut yo' ass up," Jerome barked. "When you giving me some of that good ass pussy again?" He changed his tone.

As much as I wanted to stay mad, I couldn't help but smile and cross my legs tight from my pussy tingling. This nigga had that type of effect on me, and I couldn't help it. Although I wanted to tell his ass to meet me at our spot in the next hour, I had to continue to play hard.

"Jerome please, it was already evident that you have way more of your share of bitches to fuck than just me," I scoffed.

"Man, you still tripping off that shit when old' girl came to the spot?" he asked as if it was no big deal.

"You damn right!" I yelled, sitting up in my chair.

Imani and her friends looked at me confused as to who I was talking too.

"Sorry girls," I said to them as I moved my phone from my ear.

"Who you talking too?" I heard Jerome ask me when I got back to the call.

"None of your business. Like I said, you have plenty of chicks to choose from, so you not fucking me shouldn't be an issue," I replied in a lower tone.

"You call yourself having an attitude with me because of my situation, yet you got a whole fucking family at home, and a nigga you sleep next to at night," Jerome laughed.

That shit pissed me off even more, that he can just take all of this for a fucking joke. I didn't need his ass reminding me of what I had at home.

"You can think all of this is fucking joke if you want too, Jerome. The fact is, my home life doesn't interfere with what me and you got going on. I have my shit intact while you can't control yours. I really don't have time to be dealing with your drama, Jerome, especially when I have to deal with shit on my end," I informed him.

"Ight, whatever yo," Jerome replied, then hung the phone.

Now I was even more pissed, because his ass had hung up in my face. I wasn't going to completely stop fucking Jerome, but I was going to pull back for a while just to show his ass that I wasn't one of these other lil hoes he fucks with out here. Jerome may have some bomb ass dick and head, but I still wasn't about to put up with no other muthafucka shit but my husband's. For the remainder of the afternoon I laid around the house while Imani and her friends continued to have fun.

When the evening came, Imani asked if she could sleepover to one of their houses, and I gladly let her go. After making sure she packed her bag, I gave her some money, because I never sent my child anywhere without some change in her pocket; I sent her on her way.

It was now night time, and I sprawled out across my bed catching up on Atlanta Housewives. I swear I missed my girl Nene on here, because the rest of these fake broads are boring. I heard the alarm from downstairs going off, which let me know that Ethan was home. Glancing over at the clock on the side table, I saw that it was twelve a.m. After about ten minutes, I finally heard footsteps coming up the stairs. Ethan opened our bedroom door, and looked shocked to still see me awoke.

Ignoring his presence, I continued to lay there and watch the television.

"You up late," Ethan spoke as he stood on his side of the bed and started taking off his watch.

"You home late," I responded back, still not taking my eyes off the television.

I swear this muthafucka better not push my buttons, I thought to myself. I cut my eyes over at him and watched as he placed his keys and wallet down on the table as well. He took his phone out of his back pocket and looked at it. My blood immediately started boiling.

"Damn Ethan, you staring at your phone as if you're expecting a bitch to jump out of it," I said to him.

"Please don't start, Chace. I had a long day and all I want to do is take a shower and get some sleep," he replied.

"Well, what if I wanted some dick?" I asked in a calmer tone.

I've been horny since talking to Jerome earlier, and since I was holding out on his ass, my husband would be the next best thing.

Not waiting on him to reply, I stood up on the bed on my knees, and crawled over to Ethan on the edge of his side of the bed. Unzipping his pants, I pulled his dick through the slit, and put it in my mouth. By him being gone all day, you would think he would have some type of musk on his dick from it being in his pants, but Ethan was always fresh.

"Shit," he moaned out as I took him whole in my mouth.

I had my eyes closed, and pictured that it was Jerome who I sucking off instead of dry as Ethan.

"Baby, grab my hair," I requested as I took him out of my mouth for a quick second.

Doing as he was told, Ethan grabbed a hand full of my hair and started fucking my mouth. That was the reason why I called him dry, because he rarely gave me that roughneck sex I liked; not like Jerome.

"Damn Chace, you sucking the shit out this dick!" Ethan whispered.

Grabbing ahold of his pole my hand, I began to jack it vigorously while sucking. Feeling Ethan thrusting his hips forward faster, I speeded up my pace to match his.

"Ugh!" he yelled out in a loud whisper, as he unloaded down my throat.

I continued to suck him off, not wasting a drop. Pulling back from Ethan, I turned around with my ass still up in the air, facing him, and started playing with my pussy from the back. I was beyond horny now, and my husband needed to handle this. Noticing Ethan had yet to dive in this pussy, I looked back just in time, to see his ass heading into the bathroom.

"Uh, where the fuck you going, Ethan? Yo' ass need to finish what I started," I fussed.

"Damn Chace, keep your voice down with our daughter down the hall," Ethan replied pissed.

"Imani is at a sleep over, but you would have known that had you brought your ass home at a decent our, or at least called to check on us today," I barked, with my ass still up in the air and pussy out.

"Look Chace, I'm tired baby. I promise I got you in the morning." Ethan headed back into the bathroom.

Still on all four of my fours, I couldn't believe the stunt my husband just pulled. Here I was, ass and pussy all out, gave this nigga some bomb ass head, and yet he leaves me horny and dry. My husband just actually treated me as I was some jump-off bitch! Not about to let this shit go, I jumped up from the bed and barged into the bathroom. Snatching the shower door open, I surprised Ethan as he was washing up.

"So, you mean to tell me that after I make sure that you get yours, you leave my ass hanging?" I asked him.

"Chace, I told you that I was tired!"

"You too tired to fuck your wife, but not too tired to cum in my mouth? I bet yo' ass not too tired to be talking to your bitch Kennedi though!" I threw in his face.

"Come on Chace, I thought we were pass that shit." Ethan waved me off as he slammed the shower door back shut.

Oh this nigga was tripping! I stomped back out of the bathroom and slammed the door. Walking back over to the side of my bed, I snatched up my phone, and scrolled to Jerome's name. Calling him, his ass didn't pick up. I called him again, but he still didn't pick up. I sent a text for him to call me, laid my phone back down on the table, and got into the bed.

The television was still on, but I wasn't paying that shit no attention. My phone vibrated on the table, so I snatched it back up in hopes that it was Jerome responding back to me. Instead, it was Tricia, sending me a text.

TRICIA: *Hey bitch, James came through with the info you wanted so I'm about to forward it to you now. Don't forget my bread you promised me too!*

I swear this hoe worked my nerves. When have she known me not to pay her ass when I said I would? Not trying to get into it with Tricia, because she did do as I asked of her, I simply replied back with a simple message.

ME: *OK*

Minutes later, with Ethan still in the shower, my phone vibrated again. As promised, Tricia sent me over the information that she had. After I was done looking over the message, not only had I had Kennedi's full name, but I had her address, birthday, car tag, and her social media accounts as well. Heading over to Instagram first, I searched for her name and finally got a look at the bitch who has my husband's nose wide open. I can't lie she was cute. She was light complexion, light grey eyes that were probably contacts, a slim build with a good grade of hair. Looking further down her page, I found out that she was a so-called interior decorator. This bitch's shit looked like a Rooms-To-Go showroom floor. Her color schemes even looked off brand. She did have a lot of followers, likes, and shares though. Still scooping her page out, I stopped when I ran across a post where she said she would be hitting up California within the next two weeks for a big job she was doing.

"Hold the fuck up," I said to myself as I sat up in the bed.

Looking at the date she posted the announcement, and remembering when Ethan's ass told me that he had to go to California on business as well for two weeks, I put two and two together. So this muthafucka thought his ass was slick. Telling me that he would be gone for business, when all along his ass would be laid up with another bitch! I heard the shower cut off in the bathroom, so I placed my phone back down and turned over on my side with my back facing his side of the bed.

Ethan came out of the bathroom and laid down beside me. He didn't even bother saying anything, cuddling with me, or even telling me goodnight. That's okay though, because if he thought he was about to take his ass across the globe to be with this basic bitch, he was in for a little surprise. It was officially game on!

CHAPTER 16

Kennedi

"Hey Bestie, what are you doing?" I asked Tasha when she picked up the phone.

"Hey Pookie. I ain't doing nothing. Was actually about to call you," she replied.

"Yeah... yeah, I don't believe you," I giggled as I moved around my kitchen.

I was in the process of whipping me up a quick sandwich for lunch. I hadn't eaten anything since earlier this morning, and even then that was only a bowl of cereal. It's now well after three in the afternoon and I was starving. Reaching into the pantry, I grabbed a loaf of bread and chips, and sat them both on the counter. I do the same with the lunch meat, and mayo.

"Swear." She laughed along. "I was calling to make sure you made it safe to Cali."

"Oh no, I haven't even left yet. My flight isn't until the morning."

"Really? I thought you said you were leaving today. That just goes to show that my mind be all over the place. Anyway, are you excited about your project?"

"I am, but I'm more excited about spending time with

Ethan." I smiled as I added a little bit of mayo to each of my pieces of bread. I was slapping that shit on quick as hell trying to hurry up so that I could eat.

"Don't tell me my bestie is falling in love."

"No, I wouldn't call it all that but I definitely like him," I told her honestly. "He's different though, and I'm looking forward to see where this goes."

"Well, that's good. I'm glad that you're done with Mook's dumb ass," Tasha spat.

Although he was her step-brother, she couldn't really stand Darnell anymore. After all of the things that he had done to me, I can't even lie, because I don't blame her. Many times she'd gone weeks without speaking to him, all because he'd gotten caught cheating once again. Over and over she told me to leave him alone but I wouldn't listen. Needless to say, she's happy that I'm done with him now.

"Girl yes!" I shook my head. "Speaking of his special ass. Why he called me talking crazy the other day?"

"Oh Lord, what did he say this time?"

After taking a bite of my now finished sandwich, I chewed it as if I hadn't eaten in days. Finally, I reply.

"Talking about he's trying to be nice, but I keep playing with him, and if I keep on, he's going to show me how he

166

gets down. Saying he should pop me in the mouth or something
like that."

"Girl, shut the fuck up!" Tasha yelled. "I know the hell Darnell ain't say no shit like that."

"Yes the fuck he did. This was after I went off on his ass and told him to leave me the hell alone," I told her with my mouth full of food.

"When did he get gangsta? Betta sit his ass down somewhere before he end up getting his head cracked."

"That ain't even all," I revealed. Taking a seat at the kitchen table, I pop a potato chip into my mouth. "He called me all out my name, claimed that I thought I was the shit because of my little *funky ass job*, and that I shouldn't forget that I was broke not too long ago. Then the muthafucka hung up in my ear," I snorted.

"I know you lying!" Tasha exclaimed. "That nigga has really lost his damn mind. Last I checked, you're job payed better than his, and when the hell have you ever been broke?"

"That's what the hell I was trying to figure out."

"Don't let his retarded ass get to you," Tasha advised. "Just wait until I talk to that bitch. Now I'm really looking forward to coming home. Swear I'm going to set his ass straight. Let's see how bad he is then."

"I already know how you are, so don't even do it," I told her thinking about just how left things can go when she's upset. "It's not worth it. Shit, he's not worth it. I'm just going to ignore him like I've been doing. I don't want you in trouble behind his dumb ass."

"I hear you, and you're right" Tasha agreed. "I'm still going to give that bastard a piece of my mind. How he gone call you talking crazy, when he's the one who fucked up? He wasn't thinking about making things right when he was out fucking around and being a hoe!" she yelled.

"I know, but I ain't trying to figure that out anymore. Instead, I finally cut my losses and moved on."

"I know that's right. Enough about his stupid ass. Tell me what are you're plans for the next two weeks with your boo."

After filling my best friend in on all the nasty things I planned to do, we spent the next hour on the phone laughing and talking about different things. I don't think I'd laughed that much in a while, but that's exactly how it is when Tasha and I talk. She's tough and will kick ass I a minute, but she's also silly as hell. She can literally turn anything into something funny; which is one of the reasons why I love it when she's around. Before we hang up, we promise one another that we'll find a way to meet up once I come back from California. Now off the phone, I put all of the food away, and clean my kitchen. Once I'm finished, I make my way into my bedroom and go over my luggage once last time, so I don't have to do it in the

morning.

*****

"Heyyyyy baby," I squealed as I jumped into Ethan's arms as soon as I opened the door. I wrapped my arms and legs around him, while I squeezed him tight; inhaling the scent of his cologne.

He had just gotten to the hotel, after catching a car from the airport. When he called and told me that he as on his way, I was so excited that I could barely contain myself. It had only been an hour since I had made it here myself, so I was still in the process of unpacking all of my things and hanging it all up. With me due to stay for two weeks, I didn't plan on living out of my suitcase for the entire time. As soon as we hung up I hurried up and put all the rest of the shit away. Since I had a little time to spare once I was done before Ethan made it to the hotel, I took a quick shower and got dressed in something comfortable and cute while I prepared for my man to arrive.

With me still in his arms Ethan gave me a quick twirl before he planted a big, juicy kiss on my lips. Breaking our smooch, he stared at me for a seconds without saying anything.

"Damn, I've missed you," he finally spoke.

"I've missed you too." I smiled, meaning it. I knew I missed him before, but it was not until that very moment that I realized just how much.

Again he leaned in for a kissed. Ethan's tongue snaked deeply into my mouth, and I gladly accepted it. I rubbed all over his bald head while he gripped and massaged my ass cheeks through the thin summer dress I was wearing. Pulling his lips away I titled my head backwards while he proceeded to kiss me sensually all over my neck. A low moan escaped my mouth and my eyes rolled closed. Seconds later, Ethan used his chin to nudge down the top of my dress, before he leaned down to place my left nipple into his mouth. *Thank God I decided not to wear a bra,* I thought as I enjoyed the feeling of his tongue. Simultaneously, he slid my panties to the side and plunged his finger deep into my now dripping wet honey pot. I arched my back to give him better access, while I grinding down on his finger; all while moaning in ecstasy. I was right on the verge of coming when I heard a sound that caused my eyes to pop open.

It's then that I realized that we were so caught up in the moment that neither of us noticed that we were still standing in the freaking doorway of my room. Quickly, I climbed down from Ethan's grasp and straightened out my dress so that my breast was no longer exposed. With his suitcase in hand, Ethan stepped inside and hurriedly closed the door behind him. We were both able to get inside without seeing whoever it was that was coming down the hall.

"Well, that was intense," he laughed while he placed his suitcase down on the floor.

"You don't say," I shook my head, still embarrassed at the thought of almost getting caught. "Have you checked into your room yet?" I quickly changed the subject.

"Yeah, I did that before I came up. I'm in room three-thirteen, which is right down the hall."

"Good. That means we're close."

"Not as close as I want to be," Ethan spoke as he licked his lips and looked over at me lustfully.

"Is that right? Well, let's see what we can do about that." I smirked.

Reaching behind my neck I untied the halter part of my dress, and allowed it to fall and uncover my breast. I then slid it down my body, and kicked it across the room. Now clad in nothing but a pair of black lace Victoria Secret boy shorts and peep toe sandals I removed the band from my hair and placed it on my wrist, before I shook the ponytail loose. As it fell down past my shoulders and down my back, I struck a pose. I wasn't the least bit ashamed of my body because it looked damn good. I worked hard to keep my shape in great condition, and I wasn't afraid to show it off.

"You're so fucking sexy," Ethan groaned removing his blazer.

He watched me as he undid the buttons on his shirt next. While I waited for him to undress, I decided to mess with his head a bit. Using both my hands I cupped my breast and started to massage them gently. My nipples were hard as rocks. Leaning my head down I stuck my tongue out and flicked it across my right one, which made Ethan go crazy. Letting go of his now loosened belt, he rushed over to me and picked me up in his grasp. Again, I wrapped my arms and legs around his body. Carrying me further into the room, Ethan kissed me roughly as we got closer to the bed. Once we were right in front of it he laid me down with him still in between my legs.

Since it had been weeks since the last time Ethan and I had been together, I was more than ready for him to give it to me the way only I knew he could. After our lip lock was broken, he began to trail soft, wet kisses down my neck and towards my chest. I moaned when he licked my nipple and slipped it into his mouth. With his hands now around my waist, Ethan lifted me up and scooted me back more onto the bed. I reached behind me and grabbed one of the pillows and placed it behind my head. I was ready for exactly what I knew was about to happen. Tracing his tongue around my belly ring, Ethan journeyed further until he got to my southern region.

I already knew that my panties were soaking wet, because I could feel my juices leak out of my special place, and down my ass. This was confirmed when Ethan removed the boy shorts and looked up at me in amazement.

"Goddamn, you wet as fuck," he told me with wide eyes. "That pussy leaking."

Without saying anything else, he stuck out his tongue and licked up and down my sweet spot slowly. I jerked and whimpered when I felt it brush against my clit. Ethan must have felt it too because he looked up at me and gave me a sneaky grin before slightly lifting my legs and going to work. My mouth formed into an "O" shape and my eyes rolled into the back of my head as he attacked my pussy like a starved man, alternating from licking to sucking. When he slipped two fingers into the mix, I damn near lost it! I was grinding my hips and moaning all loud like we weren't inside of a hotel. I'm sure the people in the rooms around us could hear me and knew what was going on, but at the moment I didn't give a shit.

While his fingers continued to stroke me from the inside, Ethan latched onto my clit with his mouth and started to beat on it like it was a drum and he was the soloist performing in front of millions of people.

"Oh my God!" I screamed. "What are you doing to me?"

Of course he didn't answer, just continued to drive me crazy.

Sitting up on my elbows, I looked down at him but couldn't open my mouth to speak any words. We locked eyes and I swear at that moment Ethan looked sexier than ever. He had absolutely not shame as he munched on my hot box like his favorite flavor was inside and he was trying desperately to get it out. Using my elbows, I lift my hips up off of the bed and pushed down on his tongue, just as he snaked it in and out of my now throbbing hole. This is only maybe the third time that Ethan has eaten my pussy so the entire experience is still new to me. Although I've hadn't had it done much, there's no doubt in my mind that it's now one of my favorite parts of sex. I could literally get this shit done numerous times a day. As I continued to watch Ethan move his head and mouth with precision, I swore that he was a master at this shit. Only a few seconds pass before I can't take it anymore and jerk backwards back onto the bed.

"Shit... shit!" I panted, feeling the tingle take over my body. "I'm about to cum, baby. Please don't stop. Right there," I whimpered, praying that he listened that kept doing exactly what it is that he's doing.

As if on que, Ethan sped up his pace, which I wasn't even sure was possible. My heart was beating rapidly, my legs

began to shake, and I completely lost all control of myself.

"Fuck!" I yelled locking my legs around his head and allowing the feeling to overtake me.

Ethan attacked my clit relentlessly while I trembled and flopped around the bed like a water staved ass fish. The feeling was amazing. My entire body was sensitive, as I flooded his mouth with my womanly juices. Ethan didn't seem to mind, because he continued to lick and suck it all out. One would think that the taste was something that he couldn't get enough of because he actually seemed to enjoy it. I swear I even heard him moan. With my legs still slightly locked around his head, I attempted to scoot back from his mouth. I had just finished a powerful orgasm and with my clit being so sensitive, Ethan still flicking his tongue it was more than I could take. Not letting me get away, he slid his arms up under my body and locked my legs in place.

"Ahhhh!" I hollered, but kept on licking. "Okay… okay, please stop!" I cried out, but again Ethan didn't let up.

Reaching down, I attempted to push his head back, but he just wouldn't budge. It was like he wasn't trying to hear shit I was saying. Just as I opened my mouth to yell something else, another orgasm snuck up and ripped through my body, forcing me to fall backwards and onto to pillow once again.

"Shiiiiiiiittttt!" I screamed.

One hand grabbed at the bedsheets under me and gripping them tightly in my grasps, while the other went straight to my head. I swear my eyes crossed hard as hell and I damn near snatched a bald patch out of my hair out in the front. I didn't know what the hell this nigga was doing to me, but if I died right now I would be one happy ass woman. After once again licking up everything my pussy spit out, Ethan finally pulled his face away. Using his hand, he wiped away any left over juices and stood up. Now with my vision back to normal, I stared up at him while breathing hard. I was gone, and I could tell that he knew it by the sly smirk on his face. I wanted to say something, but I wasn't ready to speak just yet. Had to get my mind right first.

"Damn girl, you would have thought a nigga was killing you in here," Ethan chuckled.

I breath deeply for a few more seconds before I reply, "It's because you were. I asked you to stop," I told him before lazily kicking my foot out in his direction. I was no where near my mark but he got the point.

"Yeah, I know. I wasn't ready yet. Had to make sure you were good."

"I was good the first time," I giggled before I sat up on the bed. Sliding the hair tie from my wrist, I pull my now damp and messy locks back into a ponytail. "Now come here and let

me make sure that you're good," I purred.

"That's what the fuck I'm talking about," Ethan smiled.

I smirked as crawled to the foot of the bed where he stood. My legs were still shaky as hell from those two powerful orgasms but I wasn't about to tell him that. No, I was going to play it cool because I had to job to do. As I slid his pants and briefs to the floor, I licked my lips. I wasn't sure what he was used to, but I was bout to suck the life out of him; just as he'd just done me. Ethan was about to see that he wasn't the only one capable of making somebody tap out.

CHAPTER 17

Chace

I paced the hospital floor, nervous as hell. I didn't mean for things to get this far, but this shit was all Ethan's fault. Had he not run his ass out of the house claiming that he was going to California for some fucking business, when he was really going to be with his side bitch, this could have all been prevented. I was already pissed at his ass for that stunt he had pulled with not fucking me the other night. So, I woke up that following morning and demanded that his ass cancel or reschedule his so-called trip because of Imani. I made up a big ass lie telling him how Imani comes crying to me when he isn't around, and how she's always asking why her daddy doesn't love her. Of course, Ethan swore me down that it wasn't true, and that he makes sure to show and let Imani know just how much he loves her. Not once did the bastard mention me in any of that equation. Never the less, his ass still left.

Now, usually when Ethan would leave to go out of town, that would be my free time with Jerome, but this time was totally different. For one, Jerome's ass was still on my shit list, so I wasn't really fucking with him right now. Then, the fact that I actually knew the real reason behind this trip Ethan was taking was fucking with me. Like I said before, I didn't give a damn what I was doing on the side, Ethan didn't know shit and he was still me husband.

The morning he left, Ethan rushed from the house like our shit was on fire, and he hasn't answered any of my calls since then. He did however reply to some of my texts, which pissed me off even more. Every time I would ask Imani to call her daddy, her little grown ass would cop an attitude, so I had to knock her in her mouth to remind her that I was the momma, and what I said goes!

Unfortunately, this time, I may have gone too far.

"Mrs. Makenzie" I heard my name being called.

I looked up to see this tall, fine ass doctor walking my way. *Damn, I'd fuck the hell out of his fine ass,* I thought to myself as the doctor approached me.

"Hi, I'm Doctor Gilbert." He extended his hand for me to shake, which I obliged.

"How's my daughter, is she going to be okay?" I immediately asked him concerned.

"Your daughter is going to be fine. She does have a mild concussion, but I gave her some medicine that'll help her with her headache. So, you said that she hit her head on her dresser playing?" Doctor Gilbert asked, clarifying what I had told him earlier when we arrived at the hospital.

"Yes. I was downstairs in the kitchen fixing Imani and me

a snack, when then I heard a loud thump over my head, up the stairs. I called out to Imai, and when she didn't respond back to me, I went up to her room. That's when I found her lying on the floor next to her dresser" I explained again.

"Well, like I just explained, she suffered a mild concussion, but she'll be okay. I will however, have to contact Child Protective Services. It is hospital protocol to do so when a minor child is hurt outside the hospital" Doctor Gilbert informed me.

The last thing I needed right now was Child Protective Services coming in here and being all up in my damn business, and I definitely don't need them trying to question Imani.

"Is that really necessary?" I asked him.

"I'm afraid we have too Mrs. Mackenzie. They'll just ask you a couple of questions to put on their report, and that'll be it."

"Can I go see my daughter please?" I asked, ignoring what he just told me.

"Of course, right this way."

Doctor Gilbert started walking with me following behind him. As I followed him to Imani's room, I pulled out my phone and tried called Ethan again. With him not answering, I left an urgent voicemail telling him that Imai was involved in an accident, and that he needed to bring his ass home! Hanging up, I set him a text with the same message as well. When we got to Imani's room, I saw my baby laying there looking peacefully asleep with a white bandage wrapped around her head.

"You can stay with her as long as you like. The nurses will send the social worker in here once she arrives" Doctor Gilbert said before he left out of the room.

As I walked over to the bed, I began to feel bad for what I had done. I didn't mean for Imani to get hurt, but she pissed me off when I went into her room to tell her to call her daddy again, and she had the nerve to tell me that she did already, and that Ethan had told her, to tell me, to stop calling him. Not only was I embarrassed that my child had to relay the message to me, but I could have sworn Imani was grinning when she told me. So, I walked over to her little ass, jacked her up by the collar of her shirt, and threw her back against the dresser; which caused her to hit her head. When she fell on the floor, I ran over to her when I didn't see her moving. Shaking her while calling her name out at the same time, Imani started slowly trying to flicker her eyes open. Relieved that she at least breathing, I ran back down the stairs, grabbed my phone, and called 911.

When the ambulance got there, that's when I informed the EMT workers that Imani was playing in her room, and must have hit her head while doing so. Sitting in the chair next to her bed, I grabbed Imani's hand and began to cry. I know I may seem like a cold-hearted bitch sometimes, but I loved my child. If something were to happen to her based off what I had done, I would never be able to live with myself. Not to mention, my black ass would be put under the jail. Squeezing Imani's hand a little tighter, I closed my eyes and said a silent prayer.

I asked God to heal my child and relieve her from any type of pain she may be enduring right now. I also prayed that Imani wouldn't remember how she got hurt once she woke up, because I'm sure she was going to get questioned. While still praying, I jumped when I heard my phone ringing in my purse. Pulling it out, I saw that it was Ethan finally calling me back.

"It's about damn time you called me!" I barked into the phone answering it.

"Where is Imani, what happened to her?" Ethan asked in a panic.

Although I was just hurt about what I had done to my baby, I was also pissed how Ethan concern was only our daughter. It took for something to happen to Imani for me to even get a response out of his ass. This was all his fucking fault in the first place!

"Imani was playing in her room when she hit her head on

the dresser. She had to be rushed to the emergency room, and now she has a concussion. If you would have stayed your ass home in the first place like I had asked, or even answered your phone when I first called, then maybe all of this could have been prevented!" I snapped.

I saw Imani's eyes fluttering, indicating that she might be waking up. It could be coming from me being loud on the phone, but at this point I didn't give a fuck.

"You sound so damn stupid right now, Chace! I'm on my way back into town. Which hospital are you at?"

"We're at South Presbyterian." With that said, I hung up the phone in his face.

Looking back over at Imani, I saw that she was now completely awake, and staring at me.

"Hi baby." I said to her in a sincere tone, as I grabbed her hand again. "How are you feeling?"

"My head hurts a little" Imani responded in a low tone.

Staring at her innocent face, all I saw was Ethan looking back at me. My daughter was every spit of her father, and most times, I detested it. But now, all I could think about was making sure that Imani and my story matched before these nosey muthafuckas started coming in here and asking her questions.

"Baby, do you remember how you got hurt?"

Imani stared at me for a little while, with a confused look on her face.

"I'm not sure mommy. I know that I was in my room, and now I'm waking up here. What happened?" Imani asked.

Thank God! "I'm not sure what you were doing upstairs, but I heard a loud sound downstairs from the kitchen. When I came up to your room, I saw you lying on the floor. You must have hurt your head while playing" I responded, lying of course.

"I want my daddy" Imani started to whine.

Ain't this some shit? I'm the one that's here with her, by her side when she woke up, and she wants her damn daddy. All the guilty feelings that I had previously had, was now officially out the window. Especially since Imani didn't remember how she got hurt, so I was in the clear with that. Taking a deep breath, I had to calm down before I snapped on Imani.

"Your daddy is on his way here from out of town. I'm not sure when he will get here exactly, but he'll be here" I responded.

For the remainder of the day, I sat next to Imani's bedside while she drifted in and out of sleep. Child Protective Services did come in and ask questions. Imani was asleep at the time that they came, which was even better. Later on that evening when the doctor came in to check on her while doing his rounds, he also informed me that by Imani having a mild concussion, that she might not remember certain things. The next morning, Ethan finally strolled his ass into the hospital. At first, he acted as if I wasn't there, with him just only speaking to the doctor and asking him questions. All the while, I stayed quiet, trying to stay calm while I still remained by Imani's bed side.

When Imani saw her father, her whole world lit up. I continued to just stand in the background, this time fuming with jealously. Their bond was like no other, and while Ethan loved Imani with every fiber in him, I could feel his love slipping away from me.

"I need to speak to you privately Chace." Ethan announced as he walked out of the hospital room and into the hall.

Following behind him, I stood against the wall with my arms folded across my chest, waiting to hear what bullshit Ethan had to say to me.

"Why weren't you watching Imani, Chace?" he had the audacity to ask me.

"The nerve of yo' ass to question me, when you didn't want to keep yo' ass home in the first place! Had you not been chasing pussy across the fucking globe, then maybe you would have been able to see about your own child!" I threw in his face.

"Here you go with the bullshit. I told you that I was away on business," Ethan proclaimed.

"Nigga, you really need to cut the shit! I already know about you and that fake ass, interior decorator hoe Kennedi! You don't think I know about her going to California, and you following right behind her ass?" I pulled my phone from my back pocket, went on Instagram, scrolled to her page and stopped on her post she made about taking the trip. Pushing the phone up to Ethan's face so that he can see exactly what I was talking about, I could tell by his sudden nervousness that his ass was busted. "Now what you not about to do, is stand yo' stupid ass there, and continue to lie to my face!' I spat.

"Um, I'm going to need you two to keep it down, or take this conversation outside."

I looked behind Ethan to see one of Imani's nurse standing there. This bitch stayed trying to come into Imani's room every chance she got since Ethan got here. Hell, she probably wanted to fuck him too!

"Girl, shut the fuck up and mind your business!" I snapped on her.

Turning my attention back to Ethan. "You better end whatever the fuck this shit is you got going on, or I will."

Rolling my eyes at the nosey ass nurse, I stormed down the hallway to leave. Ethan was steady calling out my name, but I kept walking. I really didn't plan on unleashing what I knew so far to him, but that bastard was acting as if his shit didn't stink, and the fact that I knew that he was lying made it worse. Making it to the garage, I found my car and jumped inside. Placing my head back on the headrest, I let out a frustrated sigh.

Before this, I was never worried about any outside bitch my husband fucked with. Not only was I not threatened, but I also had the confidence to know that his ass wasn't going anywhere. Now, I'll be the first to admit to myself that I might be a little worried. I mean, I still don't see Ethan leaving me for this Kennedi bitch, but I do know that he must have some type of deep feelings for her; he maybe even loved her. Pulling my phone back out, I did what I would always do every time I needed to release some frustration; I called Jerome.

"Yeah," he answered the phone.

I swear it irritated me when he did that shit, but I wasn't trying to get into it with him either.

"I need to see you" I announced.

"Oh, now you wanna see me when a nigga was trying to call you up and see you a few weeks back, you were acting funky" Jerome replied.

"Come on, Jerome. I just need to chill and relax right now. Let's just meet up."

"Ight," he finally agreed.

"You got some weed?" I asked him smiling as I cranked up my car.

"You already know I stay with a stash. What type of question is that to ask me?"

"I'm just making sure. I'll see you at the spot in twenty." Hanging up the phone, I pulled out of the parking garage, and headed to my destination.

I know any other mother in my shoes right now would still be at the hospital by her daughter's bedside, but fuck that. Imani wanted her daddy so fucking much, so she had who she wanted with her. Besides, if I would have stayed around Ethan's lying ass a minute longer, I promise you he would have been admitted to a room in that hospital his damn self.

After thirty minutes, due to traffic, I pulled up to the condo. Noticing that Jerome's car wasn't out there, I got out and let myself inside. Since he wasn't here yet, I decided to take a quick shower to freshen up. Going into the bathroom, I cut the shower on hot and stripped out of my clothes. Stepping inside, I let the water beat down on my entire body. Normally I wouldn't allow my hair to get wet since I just got a fresh sewn, but I didn't care. I felt like all the stress that I was feeling was being washed away. I jumped when I heard the shower curtain being snatched open. I opened my eyes to Jerome's sex ass standing there naked, waiting for me. His chiseled-out chest that was covered with tattoos, and his six pack caused my pussy to pulsate. Directing my eyes down to his dick that was hanging, I licked my lips.

"Damn, you couldn't wait?" Jerome asked me as he stepped behind me inside the shower.

Before I could respond, he cupped my breast from behind. Feeling his touch, I laid my head back on his chest and closed my eyes once again. I then felt Jerome's hand massaging my pussy. Between the hot water still beating down on my body, and Jerome playing with my pussy and breast, I was on fire!

Not able to take it anymore, I turned around and pushed him up against the wall. Dropping down to my knees, I took him whole into my mouth. It's been a minute since I tasted his juices, so I was about to suck this nigga dry! Placing both of my hands on his dick, I went to work. I was sucking and slurping, while Jerome moaned out loud and pulled on my hair. When I felt him speeding up his pace, I knew that he was about to cum. Sucking on his dick harder, Jerome screamed out as he unloaded his seeds all down my throat. In the beginning of us fucking around, I would never allow him to cum in my mouth, because I felt that my husband was the only man I would do that too, but obviously things have changed, and now Jerome gets the full treatment.

Pulling me up by my shoulders, Jerome switched positions with me, and was now the one on his knees in front of me with my right leg up on his shoulder. Soon as I felt his tongue sucking on my clit, I lost it! Jerome began to feast on my pussy as if he was trying to win some fucking money in a best eating pussy contest! Grabbing ahold on the wall, so that I could maintain my balance, I closed my eyes and enjoyed this feeling. This was exactly what I needed.

Jerome and I took it from the shower to the bed, where we fucked for about two hours. Once we were done, we were so damn sweaty that we had to actually take a shower this time. Once we were done, we both laid naked in the bed passing a blunt between the both of us.

"Aye, you still talk to that chick Tricia?" Jerome asked me as he passed the blunt back over to me.

I took a long pull, held it for a few, and then released it before answering him. "Off and on, why?" I replied.

"I was up in Club Onyx with my boys and your brothers the other night, and she was up in there with a few of some other thot hoes. Anyway, she approached me and asked if I could buy her and her friends some drinks, so I didn't mind. Then, the hoe tried to chill in VIP with us, and when I had the security deny her entrance in our section, lil momma started tripping" Jerome said.

"What you mean tripping?"

"Man, she started yelling, and cursing. Then, she had the nerve to say how I was whipped on your married pussy, which is why I wouldn't let her in the section. She called out your name and all. After her raggedy ass was thrown out of the club, your brothers turned to me and asked me what was up" Jerome explained.

"What did you tell them?" I asked sitting up.

"Shit, you already know how I don't like my business in the streets, so I told them that her ass ain't know what the fuck she was talking about."

"Did they believe you?" I asked in a panic.

"I doubt it, because after that, they both kept eyeing me the rest of the night. You need to handle that loud mouth hoe Tricia, and holler at your brothers as well. You know that's how I get my main bread by working for them, so I'm not about to fuck that up for nobody" Jerome expressed.

This was new news to me, because my brothers nor Tricia never mentioned any of that going down. Tricia, I can handle, but my brothers were another story. This was now all just some extra, unnecessary shit added on my list for me to deal with.

CHAPTER 18

Kennedi

"Oh my God, Ethan! Is she alright?" I asked in a panic.

"Yes, she's doing fine now. Thank God," he replied. "I was so worried on my flight back. I couldn't even think straight."

"I can only imagine," I sighed. "Hold on one second, Ethan," I said when I heard someone knocking on the door. "Who is it?" I asked placing the phone at my side.

"Room service," A male's voice on the other side said.

Climbing out of the bed, I made my way over to the door. After standing on my tippy toes, and seeing that it was indeed a hotel employee, I opened the door.

"Hello, Ma'am. You ordered the Korean fried chicken wings, buttermilk mashed and grilled asparagus?" the guy asked.

"Yes I did. You can put it over there." I pointed towards the dining area. Walking over to my purse, I reached inside and grabbed a ten-dollar bill before meeting him back at the door. "Thank you." I smiled handing him the tip.

"Your welcome, Ma'am, and thank you."

"OK, sorry. That was my food," I spoke, putting the phone back against my ear.

"It's okay, baby. I know you gotta eat," Ethan groaned. "I wish I was still there with you."

"No worries. We'll do it again," I assured him taking a seat on the couch. "So, what did she say happened?"

"The same dumb ass shit she said when I was there. Talking about Imani was playing in her room and hit her head on the dresser. That shit doesn't even sound right to me," he huffed. "Then she tried to pin the shit on me talking about it wouldn't have happened if I wouldn't have come to Cali or answered my phone. What the hell does either of those things have to do with my daughter hitting her head? If it was an accident, then it would've happened if I was here or there or am I crazy?" Ethan asked.

"No," I spoke up. "You're not crazy, your right. Do you think that…" I paused. "You know what, never mind."

"What?"

"It's nothing?"

"Don't do that, Kennedi. Tell me what's on your mind?" Ethan urged.

"I was just wondering if maybe your ex may have hurt your daughter because you left. It would make sense as to why she's saying that if you would have stayed back home she wouldn't be hurt."

"Nah, I don't think Chace would hurt Imani. Especially

not because she's mad at me," he responded, even though he didn't sound completely sure.

"OK, I was just wondering because her wording sounded strange, that's all." I shrugged.

"Yeah, I get it." There was a slight pause before Ethan said, "Well, let me get going. Baby girl is being discharged and I want to spend some time with her today. I'll call you later and we'll talk more, alright?"

"Sounds good. I hope she feels better. I'll talk to you later."

"Will do."

After we both hang up, I get up from the the couch and make my way into the kitchen to wash my hands. Once I'm done, I take a seat at the dining room table, and start eating my food. As I chow down on the delicious meal that was prepared just for me, I started to wonder if what I'd said about Ethan's ex hurting his daughter had upset him. Although I wasn't trying to make him mad, what I said did make sense; at least to me anyway. I would hope that I was wrong, and a woman would never hurt her child over a man, but these days you just never know. Watching the news has showed me that the world is a crazy place and sometimes people do things that you would never expect them to do. Hopefully Ethan's not upset but if he is, I'm not going to apologize about something that he damn near drug out of me. I wasn't going to say anything, but he wanted to know what was on my mind so I told him.

Twenty minutes later I was stuffed, up out my chair and pushing the cart back out into the hallway. I'm not sure what they did to those chicken wings but they were damn good. The mashed potatoes were not the best so I'm going to pass on those next time, but the asparagus were decent. After closing and locking the door, I walked into my bedroom, flopped down on the bed and crawled up to the top of it. Once I wiggle around a bit, I was finally able to get the blankets up and over me, and when I do I just lay there. I'm bored as hell right now. I have four days left of my stay and there's literally nothing left for me to do. I wrapped up my job this morning, and of course my client loved it. She adored her bedroom so much that she plans on having me do a few more jobs in the near future, and even promised to refer me to some of the other basketball wives. I was so excited when she said that that I jumped on girlfriend and hugged her tight as hell. No doubt I was instantly embarrassed, but she didn't mind. In fact, she laughed and hugged my crazy ass right back because she was just as excited as I was, but for her new sleeping space. I've done a lot of jobs over the years, but this one has been by far the best.

Now, with four days to go, I'm trying to come up with something to do with myself. At first I planned to spend the rest of my downtime with Ethan but he got called away when his daughter was hospitalized yesterday. While I feel sorry for his baby girl, I'm kind of feeling bummed because we were having so much fun while he was here. We went shopping, a few club spots where we danced and had a few drinks, and out to eat at some of the restaurants. I'd be lying if I said that we didn't spend most of our time holed up in my room making love. We definitely made up for lost time, and I loved every minute of it.

Rolling over, I reach over on Ethan's side of the bed for his pillow. Bringing it up to my nose I inhale deeply. The smell of his scent forces me to close my eyes and right away an image of him and that bald head, the way he looks at me, that perfect smile, and all of our nights together began to replay in my mind. After a few moments of mentally reliving those moments, I pop my eyes back open and drop his pillow back on the side of the bed while breathing hard. Shaking my head, I can't help but smile. I don't know what that man has done to me, but it's definitely something. Here he is over eight hundred miles away, and still he has the ability to make me feel this way. My temperature has gone up a few degrees and my pussy is pulsating, and it's all just off of his smell alone.

"Shit," I say sitting up in the bed. "Let me get my ass up and do something with myself before I go crazy in here."

Climbing out of the bed, I head over to the desk area and take a seat. After powering on my MacBook, I go directly to my emails to see what business I may have to attend to. There are a few inquires about quotes for services that I plan to get to, as well as some for other things, but there is one in particular that I'm looking for. I continue to scan the many messages, bypassing all the ones that don't really matter to me at the moment. After a few minutes, I finally find the one that I'm looking for. When I open it and read the message that was sent, a huge smile graced my face and I start to do a little dance in my seat. *Hell yeah.* It says that my order will be complete, and able to be picked by next week. That is truly music to my ears.

With my parents twenty-fifth anniversary coming up, I wanted to make sure to do something special for the two of them. Not only did I treat them to a seven-day cruise to Europe, but I also ordered them a large portrait oil painting of their wedding picture to put up in the family room over the fireplace. I know they are going to love it, and I can't wait.

On top of all of that, I've planned a little dinner party, that neither of them know nothing about. I've paid caterers and everything. It's going to be nice. Of course I didn't go all out, because that's not something either of them would have wanted, just something small, and intimate. Something with just their friends. I'm sure they will enjoy it though.

An hour later when I'm finished returning all of the emails that I'd received, I'm once again bored. Glancing out of the window, I see that the sun is just about to go down. Normally when I'm out of town I'd be trying to think of somewhere to go, but since I've never been here and don't know anyone out this way, I'm going to stay my ass inside. Grabbing my phone, I scroll through it aimlessly. With nothing else to, I decide to check out social media. My first stop is Instagram. Since becoming so popular from my designs my page is up to more than seven-hundred-thousand followers and because of that I usually have so many comments that it's hard to read them all. Even if I did, it's literally impossible to reply to everybody so I don't even try to. Instead I try to catch the few that I can and keep it moving.

I plop down on the couch twenty minutes later still bored out of my damn mind. Going to the call logs, I tap on Tasha's mobile number and wait for it to ring.

"Hey boo, what you doing?" I ask as soon as she answers.

"Hey Pookie. I ain't doing nothing, but just getting in from the library."

I laughed, "I bet you were studying."

"You know it," Tasha replied as she giggled. "What's up with you, and how are you enjoying Cali?"

"It's cool. I'm bored as hell though."

"Why? I thought your boo was there with there with you. Did he do something to you?" she asked in a different tone. One that let me know that was ready to kick Ethan's ass if need be.

"Calm down killa," I cracked up. "No, he didn't do anything to me. He had to go home because his daughter had an accident. Apparently she fell while upstairs playing in her room, and ended up with a concussion."

"Damn, is she alright?"

"Yeah, she's fine. Ethan had to rush home though, and now I'm sitting here for the next four days all by my damn self," I whined. I could hear Tasha laughing on the other end of the phone.

"Yo' spoiled ass," she cackled.

"Shut up heffa."

"I'm saying though. His daughter busted her damn head bad enough to end up in the hospital, and you're sitting there pouting because you gotta be in Cali by yourself." She was laughing so hard, I couldn't help but to join in. Tasha was so damn silly. "You crazy as hell man, I swear."

"She wasn't even hurt though, Tasha." I rolled my eyes. "Swear I think that bitch did the shit on purpose just so she could get him away from me and have him come home. The shit just doesn't even make sense to me."

"Girl, I hope you playing right now, because I hope that a mother wouldn't do no shit like that to her own child." There was silence for a few seconds before Tasha spoke again. "But shit, you just never know these days. Some of these hoes be crazy over a nigga. But still, I hope she didn't do that, because that would be so fucked up."

"Yeah, it would be," I agreed.

"My next question is, if she did, why the hell would she be on some dumb shit like that? If her and Ethan aren't together, what would be the point?"

I sat thinking for a minute. "I'm not sure, but from what he's told me, she's been dating herself. He also said that she was petty and immature as hell, so I don't really know."

"Humph," she snorted. "She can be all of the above, but she better keep that shit in New York. I'd hate to have to drag that bitch for acting up, and fucking ya man up for allowing the shit to happen."

"Yeah, hopefully it's nothing. I don't really know what's going on, so I can do is believe what he says. At least until I find out something different."

"I guess you're right."

"Anyway, enough about me. What's going on with you?"

"Umm, I'm almost done with my finals, so I'll be coming home soon."

"Oh my God, I can't wait!" I shouted, truly happy that I was going to be able to see my best friend. It's been a few months since we've last seen one another due to both of our busy schedules and a face to face was definitely needed.

"Yep, and I'll be there for a little over a month," she told me, and I could tell that she was smiling.

"Hell yeah, I'm definitely taking some time off. We are going to have a blast! I'm talking, getting into all kinds of trouble."

"Oh shit, speaking of trouble," Tasha blurted. "I was talking to my mother earlier today, and she started talking about Mook." Just hearing her mention his name made my stomach turn but I didn't say anything. Instead I allowed Tasha to keep on with her story. "She was telling me that he's been in jail for the last few days after going to court for an indictment he got on a drug charge. Well, when he went downtown on his court date the judge gave him a high bail. Supposedly it was like twenty grand or something like that, and since nobody paid to get him out he had to sit in there until his next court date."

"I knew it," I spoke up. "He's so fucking hardheaded."

"He told you about it?"

"Yeah, he did. He called me a few weeks ago."

"I bet you he didn't tell you this," Tasha vowed. "I know he didn't tell you that the drugs they found in his car were his."

"Girl, shut the fuck up!" I exclaimed. "When the hell did Mook start selling drugs?" This was news to me. Last I heard he was still working at the same place.

"That's the point. He's not selling shit. The nigga is smoking it."

"What?!" My chin hit my damn chest at that news. I couldn't believe it. Darnell was doing drugs? "Are we talking about weed, or crack?" I asked, because I needed to know.

"Both."

"I know you lying!"

"I swear," Tasha promised. "My momma told me that Mook started off smoking weed. Then he started lacing it, and now he's hitting the pipe. Told her it's only on occasion, but she said she knows better. You know it ain't no such thing as an occasional crackhead."

"Hell nah," I agreed.

"That's why Big Darnell hasn't been fucking with him like that. He knows his son is on that shit and he's washed his hands of him. Something about him taking some money or something like that," she informed me.

"Oh my God, this is crazy." I shook my head. "It makes sense now."

"What does?"

"The way he's been acting. Popping up at my house, basically stalking me and talking all crazy and shit. The nigga is gone off them fucking drugs." A chill ran down my spine.

All this time I was thinking Darnell was just tripping. I figured he was harmless and just acting up, and here I was dealing with a fucking junkie. Who knew what he was capable of now that he was messing with the more hardcore shit? For the next ten minutes Tasha and I continued to talk about Darnell and what he had going on in his life. I ain't gone lie. I kind of felt bad for him. It's one thing to be caught up in some shit, but it's another to be a drug addict. I'd been trying to tell him for years to stay the hell away from

Tatemville, but he wouldn't listen. Now his life is all going down hill, and I'm positive that it all stemmed from him hanging around over there. Not only is Darnel on that shit, but he might have to do some time behind it as well. If so, while I feel sorry for him, it's probably best and it'll definitely be a lesson learned.

It's sad to say, but at least I won't have to worry about him bothering me anymore. I know that may sound cruel, but it is what it is. I didn't want to deal with him before I found out that he was using, so I really ain't trying to fuck with him now. Don't want that type of druggie shit anywhere near me. After chopping it up with my bestie for a little longer, we said our goodbyes, promising to catch up in the next day or so.

*****

It's almost four o'clock in the morning, and I'm still lying in the bed wide awake. After smashing that pizza and chicken wings, I just knew that with a full belly I would be knocked out from itis, but nope even that didn't happen. Instead I continued to sit here and watch episode after episode of both The Fresh Prince, as well as George Lopez. Social media is a bust, and nobody is awake this time of night, so basically I'm on my own. It's just me, this bed, and this big bag of Doritos that I got room service to bring me. Where they got it from, I'm not sure, nor do I care; as long as they got it. The way they taste, it was well worth the twenty bucks that I spent, including the tip. On top of snacking like I ain't got no sense, I've also taken a hot bubble bath, and still nothing. I guess my mind isn't tired yet. Whenever that happens I'll go to bed, but until then I'm up.

The chiming of my phone get's my attention. It's the text message alert, and immediately I wonder who in the world would be texting me this early in the morning. With curiosity getting the best of me, I lean over towards the nightstand and pick it up. When I see Ethan's name flash across the screen, my heart beat speeds up. Licking my cool ranch fingers clean, I wipe them clean on my shirt, and unlock my phone. Heading to my messages, I anxiously read what he wrote.

ETHAN: *I'm sure that you're probably asleep right now, but you crossed my mind. Imani had all of my attention today, which is why I didn't call you back as promised. We'll talk tomorrow. Goodnight Beautiful.*

I smiled as I read his message. Funny thing is, I'd honestly forgotten that he was supposed to call me back, but it's nice to know that he hadn't. Although I wasn't sleeping like Ethan thought, I didn't reply to the text message. There was no need to. I'd speak to him later on today, just like he'd planned. It may be late in the afternoon, because I was sure once I passed out, I would be out until mid-afternoon. Just as I was about to put my phone back on the nightstand, another message came through. When I started to read this one, my heart dropped.

ETHAN: *I also wanted to let you know that I think I'm falling in love with you. No, scratch that, I KNOW that I am. I love you Kennedi Carter! I just hope this doesn't scare you off, because I'm all in, and I hope that you are too. Again, goodnight baby*

With my heart beating a mile a minute, I continued to stare down at my phone in shock and disbelief. *Did I just read what I thought I just read,* I thought to myself over and over again, even though I could see the message clear as day. My mind was all over the place. *Do I respond to the text, or should I just wait to speak to him later?* I didn't know what the hell to do, so I did nothing. Placing my phone back on the nightstand, I rolled the bag of chips up, and placed them in the drawer. I then turned off the television, because I needed complete silence. It wasn't like I was watching it anymore anyway. All I could think about now was Ethan and what he'd just said.

Pulling the covers up to my chin, I just laid in the bed staring at the ceiling. *He loves he, huh? But do I love him?* I ask myself. Honestly I don't even know. What I do know is that I like him, a lot actually. Maybe more than I care to admit. Could it be love though? I guess only time will tell. As far as being "all in" like Ethan says, I guess I am. I'm willing to ride this thing until the wheels fall off. I know that Ethan is a good man, and a good man deserves a good woman, and I believe that I'm the good woman that he needs. Before I know it, my eyes get heavy and I began to doze off. Just before I completely pass out, I smile as I think about what the future brings for Ethan and I, and at this moment, I couldn't be happier.

CHAPTER 19

Chace

It's been three weeks since Imani has been home from the hospital, and her and Ethan were working my last damn nerves with all this fucking bonding they called themselves doing. All Imani wanted was to be up under her father and literally say fuck me. Granted, I was the cause of her getting hurt in the first place, but I also was the one that got her little ass the medical attention she needed ASAP. On top of that, I missed my period this month, which already led me to believe that I was pregnant.

I know my body, and my period was like clock worth. So, when Aunt Flo didn't pay me a visit this month, I just knew my ass was pregnant; and sure enough, a home pregnancy test confirmed it last night. Now, normally a wife would be ecstatic to be having a baby from her husband, and add to their family, but this definitely wasn't the case. Not only did I not want to have a child, but I wasn't even sure who the fuck the father is!

I've been fucking both Jerome and Ethan at the same time, with no type of protection. It never crossed my mind about how reckless I was being, and could end up being pregnant. There was no doubt that I was having an abortion, and soon!

"Mommy, daddy said he's taking me shopping today and that you can come." I looked in my bedroom doorway to see Imani standing there.

I looked over at the clock on Ethan's side of the bed, and saw that it was eleven in the morning. Sucking my teeth, I rolled on my side, with my back now facing the doorway, and pulled the covers over my head; ignoring Imani. The nerve of Ethan sending her in here to invite me to go out with them, as If I was some fucking stranger. Usually, I would jump at the opportunity to shopping and burning up Ethan's black card, but I didn't have the energy.

Physically and mentally, I just wasn't there this morning. Soon as that pregnancy test came back positive, it was like my body gave off immediate symptoms. I also didn't want to risk Ethan asking me any questions as to why I would be acting so stand-offish, or moody. At this point, I just wanted to be left the hell alone.

I must have dozed back off, because I was awoken again with the covers being pulled from over my head.

"I sent Imani up here to tell you that we were going to the mall, and that you can come with us." Ethan announced standing over me on my side of the bed.

"I heard what you *told* Imani to tell me, as if you couldn't speak to me yourself, and I'm tired right now." I replied irritated.

"I didn't mean anything by asking our daughter to ask you to join us. I was just handling some business at the time I told Imani to come up here and ask you; that's all." Ethan responded, trying to sound genuine.

Little did Etan know though, I just wasn't in the mood to deal with him or Imani. The best thing they could do is get the fuck out of my presence, and stay that way for a while. I also needed for them to get out of the house, so that I could schedule my appointment to have this abortion. I just wanted to get this over with, and go back to doing me; only more careful.

"Fine, we'll be gone for most of the afternoon. Since Imani is feeling better, I figured I'd take her shopping and maybe lunch and a movie." Ethan spoke, still standing over me.

"That's fine." Was all I said as I pulled the covers back up to my chin.

Staring down at me a few seconds longer, Ethan finally left out of the room. I closed my eyes and tried to go back to sleep, but I couldn't. So, I just laid there with my eyes closed, and started thinking about where things were in my life right now. On the outside looking in, folks thought I had it the easy way.

I was married to a fine, successful man, we had a beautiful
daughter together, lived in a big ass house with expensive cars to match, and didn't have a financial care in the world. And yet, all that was nothing more than a façade of what my life was really like. My life, along with my marriage has been nothing but a lie from day one, but I still wanted to make everything work. In the beginning, I loved my husband with everything in me, which is why I did what I had done t put him through college and beyond.

Then, of course when Ethan started getting his status up, along with that came his ego, and other bitches into the picture. Over time, I just stopped caring as long as my home stayed secured. Now, I had this nagging feeling in the back of my mind about this Kennedi chick. I would never let another bitch see me sweat, but I was worried that this is one piece of pussy that had Ethan mind gone. Even though his trip was cut short, due to Imani's *accident,* I'm sure his ass was still in contact with the bitch.

I decided for now, to not bring her up to him again, because I knew all Ethan would do is lie, but I was far from just letting this shit ride. About an hour or so later, I heard the door alarm chirp upstairs, indicating that someone had gone out the front door. Assuming that it was Ethan and Imani, I got up from the bed, and looked out the bedroom window. When I saw Ethan truck backing out of the garage, I sighed a sigh of

relief as I got back in the bed.

Grabbing my phone from my night stand, I googled abortion clinics. I was looking for one that was at least an hour away from our city. I know I could have just asked Tish, since her ass stayed up in them muthafuckas, but I didn't want her big mouth ass up in my business. As I strolled through the selections from google, Jerome called my phone.

Swiping the phone over to ignore, I went back to scrolling on goggle. Jerome called right back. Sucking my teeth, I ignored the call again. Still scrolling through google, a text message came through.

J: *I know you see me calling yo ass*

ME: *Boy I'm sleep*

I replied back lying, I didn't feel like dealing with his ass either.

J: *I just saw your dude leave with yo shorty, open the door*

Standing up, I went back over to the window, and saw Jerome standing his dumb ass in front of my house. Afraid that someone will see him, I quickly ran downstairs to let him inside. I knew that Ethan and Imai would be gone for a while, so I wasn't worried about them popping back up at the house. I did however, wanted to get Jerome away from my fucking house.

"What the fuck you are doing here?" I asked as I snatched the door open.

Jerome stood there smirking, as he looked me up and down. I had forgot just that quick that I only had on a pair of lace boy shorts with a cami top. Sucking my teeth, I pulled him into the house and closed the door behind him.

"Damn, my dick just got hard as fuck looking at yo sexy ass." Jerome flirted as he grabbed me by waist, and pulled me closer to him.

The smell of his Polo cologne that he always wore, was intoxicating. My pussy got wet as I felt Jerome finger slid inside my shorts.

"Stop." I demanded as I pulled away from him. "What are you doing just popping up to my house Jerome?" I asked again as I tried to compose myself.

"Shit, I was in the neighborhood, and saw old boy pulling out, so I decided to stop by." Jerome answered with that sexy ass grin of his as he pulled me back closer to him.

This time, I couldn't fight this shit. I was horny as shit and needed to catch this nut. That's one other reason I knew I was definitely pregnant; my hormones. Whenever I was pregnant, I always wanted to fuck like a dog in heat! Kissing me on my neck, I guided Jerome to the family room.

"Bend that ass over on the couch." He demanded.

Doing as I was told. I got on the couch on my knees, and tooted my ass in the air. Not bothering to take my shorts off, Jerome pulled them to the side, and dove in my pussy.

"Oh shit!" I moaned out as I felt his thick meat open me up.

This man dick was so damn good, that he had me fucking him in my own damn house and not giving a damn.

"Damn, this pussy tight." Jerome whispered out.

I arched my back more as I began to throw the pussy back at his ass.

"Damn baby." I sang out as I felt his dick in the pit of my stomach.

Jerome grabbed a hold of my hips, and started grinding in my pussy. That shit drove me crazy! I was so wet, that I felt my juices sliding down my right leg. I had already came twice, but still wanted more. Jerome started speeding up his pace as our bodies slapped hard against one another. I could tell he was about to cum, and I wasn't ready for that.

Quickly snatching away from him, I stood up off the couch and switched positions with him. Pushing Jerome down on the couch, I straddled him. Sliding down on his thick pole, I went to work! I started riding Jerome dick as if my life depended on it. Tightening my pussy muscles around his dick,
I began to do my own grinding!

"That's right, ride that shit!" Jerome said as he slapped my ass.

Taking that as my cue, I bounced my ass up and down on his dick. I would stay up a few seconds longer, and grip the head of his dick.

"Fuck!" Jerome moaned out, as he sat up on the couch and hugged me tight.

Pumping hard into my pussy, I knew there was no way I could stop him from cuming now. Thrusting hard, Jerome finally let out a loud grunt as he exploded all up in me. If I wasn't already pregnant, I'm sure I would be after this. Still grinding, I leaned forward on him. Both of our heart beats seemed to be racing one another as they both were beating fast.

Finally, I leaned up and got off of Jerome.

"You know I don't by that *you were just in the neighborhood* bullshit ass story, don't you?" I spoke as I headed into the kitchen for a bottle of water.

"Why, 'cause you think a nigga like me don't belong in this neighborhood?" Jerome asked me as he stood up and fixed his pants.

"Exactly. So, what are you really doing at my house?" I grabbed a bottle of water out of my fridge, without even bothering to grab Jerome.

Now that I got what I wanted from him, his ass needed to go.

"Damn, you ain't gone offer me nothing to drink?" Jerome asked me as he started walking towards the kitchen.

"Jerome cut the shit and answer my question, what are you doing here?"

"Nah, for real. I had to run an errand for your brother which wasn't too far from here, so I decided to stop by when I saw yo peoples leaving." Jerome admitted.

"You know you can't be popping up like this though. I do have some nosey ass white folks as neighbors around here." I said before taking a sip of my water.

Before any one of us could talk again, my house phone started ringing. Not many people had my house number, so I went over to the phone by the kitchen island, to see who was calling. When I saw that it was my brother, Marquise number on the caller ID, I panicked.

"Oh shit, that's Marquise calling!" I said in a panic.

Jerome looked equally as nervous as I did. The phone rung two more times before I finally answered it.

"Hey Marquise." I spoke calmly into the phone.

"What's up lil sis, why you not answering your cell?" he asked.

"Because I'm downstairs, and I left it upstairs." I replied cutting my eyes over at Jerome who was still just standing there.

"Oh yea, well how about you tell that nigga Jerome I said either bring his ass out that door in the next ten seconds, or I'm coming in there to get him. Then, afterwards, I'll handle you." Marquise spoke in a low, menacing tone…

CHAPTER 20

Kennedi

Three weeks later…

"Oh my goodness!" my mother yelled as she placed her hands over her mouth in amazement.

Tears immediately pooled in her eyes, and slowly began to roll down her now flushed cheeks. Stuck in the same place, she continued to stand there, not saying anything else. She was choked up, and I knew it. This is exactly how I pictured she would be, and I loved it. This meant that my gift was perfect. My mother, father and I all stood in the middle of the family room staring at the oil painting that I'd had put up while we were at their anniversary dinner a few hours ago. As we all looked above the fire place, I couldn't help but smile. The guy who painted the picture, captured their wedding photo perfectly. It cost me a pretty penny, but it was definitely money well spent.

"I don't even know what to say," my father spoke. "It's beautiful, and I love it." The tone of his voice let me know that he too was getting choked up, which didn't happen a lot. Instead of breaking down, he turned to me and pulled me into a strong embrace. "Thank you, baby. I love it."

Looking up at him, I smiled. "You're welcome, daddy."

Now broken from my father's hug, I was immediately grabbed by my mother. She squeezed me so tight, it took my breath away. Pulling away, she held me by my shoulders and looked at me. Tears continued to spill down her face, but she didn't bother to wipe them away.

"This is amazing, and I really want to thank you," she sniffed. "You didn't have to do all of this for us, Kennedi."

"I know I didn't, Ma, but I wanted to." I smiled. "You both deserve this and so much more. You've done so much for me over the years, so it's only right that I return the favor, especially now that I can." Feeling myself getting emotional, I paused for a second to gather my emotions. Once I'm done, I lift my finger up. "I have one more gift for you both," I tell them before reaching into my bag and handing my mother an envelope. "It's just a little something to show my appreciation to you both for being such wonderful parents."

Slowly, I watch as my mother opened the sealed envelope. Once she has it opened, she pulled out the contents and started to read. When her mouth dropped open and she began to scream, my father moved closer to see what all of the excitement was all about. It was the seven day cruise to Europe, that I knew they would enjoy. I couldn't remember the last time my parents had gone on vacation together. Of course my mother had gone on a few over the years with some of her friends, but I can count on one hand how many times she's actually gone on one with my father. With him constantly working, and not wanting to take off, my mother got tired of asking. I can't say that I blame her. Now my father doesn't have any excuses of why he can't go. I've already contacted his assistant manager to set up all of the help that may be needed to run the company, so now my daddy is free and clear to go away and enjoy himself with my mom.

I spent the next two hours at my parent's house. While there they both thanked me so many times that I lost count. Each time I told them that my gifts were nothing, and that if I could, I'd give them the world, because to me they deserve it. As I said before, both of my parents have always provided for me. While they raised me together, each brought a different type of support into my life. My father worked hard to make sure that my mother and I had everything we wanted and needed, but he also instilled the value of working for the things you want. He never wanted me to have to depend on anyone, which is why he offered me the job straight out of high school. My daddy said that there weren't a lot of men like him around anymore, and because of that, he wanted me to have my own.

My mother on the other hand held down the fort. She took care of home, so she was who I spent most of my time with, because my father worked so much. She took me to school, picked me up and helped me with my homework. Not only did she help me become knowledgeable in my studies, but she taught me how to carry myself like a lady at all times. Cooking was also a skill that I needed to learn, because like she said, 'Don't no man wanna marry a woman that can't cook.' Both of my parents were strict when it came time to be, but never to the extreme. I was pretty much a laid back kind of kid, so I rarely got into trouble. Even now, I kept my nose clean and stayed out of the way. Other than work, I didn't have much time for many other things; which is why this Ethan thing is so exciting to me.

Speaking of Ethan, I didn't tell my parents a lot about him, only a few details about how we met and that we'd been seeing each other for a few weeks. I didn't bother to mention the fact that he had an ex-wife or a daughter at home, because I figured it was too soon to drop that bomb. My mother was glad that I was moving on from Darnell, while my daddy wanted to know who the man was that was trying to take his baby girl away. After promising to let them meet them both when the time was right, I kissed my parent's goodbye, and headed out the door.

*****

"So, are you going to go in there and look at it and at least

see what it says?" Tasha asked as she stared down at me as I sat on top of my bed. I didn't answer, only shrugged my shoulders. "Come on, Kennedi," she urged grabbing my arm.

"I don't want to," I whined pulling back. I was almost to the point of tears.

"Well, if you weren't going to see what it says, what was the point of buying it then?"

With my arms threw in the air, I shouted, "I don't know! I don't know anything right now."

"Just," Tasha started plopping down on the bed beside me. "calm down. Whatever it says, it's going to be alright."

"You don't know that," I sniffled glancing up to look at her while I fidgeted with my phone and rocked my legs. My mind is all over the place. "I don't know what to do right now."

Tasha gave me a warm smile. "Well, first, you gotta at least see what it says."

As if on cue a text comes through. It's Ethan. I glance down at my phone, and smile through my now fallen tears.

ETHAN: *Good afternoon beautiful. How is your day going so far?*

"It's him," I tell Tasha holding my phone up for her to see.

"Are you going to respond?"

"I don't really know what to say," I told her while I wiped my face with the back of my hand.

"So, you're just going to ignore the man?" she chuckled.

"Maybe." I shrugged, which caused her to laugh even harder.

"Yo' ass is crazy." Getting up from the bed, Tasha made her way towards the bathroom. "If you aren't going to look I am. I'm not about to sit here all day and play games with you. I didn't drive to the store for nothing." I heard as she disappeared behind the door.

Moments later she came back into to view. In between her fingers held a small white stick. I continued to sit on the bed, not moving. Wanting to know what the answer was, but to afraid to ask, I tried desperately to read Tasha's face but it was null of emotion. *Is it a yes or a no*, I thought to myself over and over again. Why the words wouldn't leave my mouth I don't know. Maybe it was because I didn't really want to know what the answer was. I guess in my mind if I pretended that this issue didn't exist I could just go on about my day as if nothing mattered. I knew better though, and I knew that I really needed to know; even though I kind of already did.

My period was supposed to come on right after I came back from California which was three weeks ago. I haven't seen it, so it doesn't take a rocket scientist to know that I could be pregnant. Add in the fact that I never remembered to get my refill for my birth control pills right before I left and that while gone Ethan and I didn't bother to use condoms. The entire time we were together in the hotel room we fucked like rabbits and not once did either of us mention protection. Thinking back, I don't know what came over me or him. I guess we were both was so caught up in the moment that protecting ourselves didn't matter. Now I could potentially be paying for that dumb ass decision, and I had no clue what I was going to do. Ethan and I are still in the beginning stages of our relationship so a baby isn't something that either of us have talked about.

"So, do you want to know what it says?" Tasha asked pulling me from my thoughts.

"Yeah, I guess I do… even though I think I already know."

"Humor me and tell me what you think."

Rolling my eyes, I shake my head and say, "It's positive isn't it?"

"Yes!" Tasha smiles.

"What the hell are you smiling for?" I asked jumping off of the bed and rushing over to her. Snatching the test out of her hand I look at the results and the words **positive** can be read as plan as day.

"My best friend is about to have a baby," Tasha sang while she bounced her shoulders. "I'm going to be an auntie."

"You are too damn chipper for me, and who's to say that I'm having a baby?" As soon as the last words left my lips, Tasha's face dropped.

"What the hell is that supposed to mean?" she asked with her hands on her hips. When I didn't say anything, she goes on. "I know you aren't saying what I think you're saying, Kennedi."

I lowered my head. "I don't know."

"I know the fuck you ain't thinking about getting an abortion."

"Maybe," I shrugged, not sure of what the hell I planned to do. At the moment I was just saying anything and trying to make sense of it all. "I can't have a baby right now."

"Don't do that. I'm not going to let you keep up with this pity party bullshit! Don't you sit there and pretend like you don't know how this happened. You laid yo' ass down like a grown woman and fucked, so you deal with this shit like a grown woman," Tasha scolded me like she was my mother.

I wasn't surprised or mad at her approach, because that's exactly how she'd always been. Tasha had my back until the very end, but she wouldn't hesitate to call me out on my bullshit when it came time to, and that was yet another reason why I loved her so much. She was a firm believer of accepting responsibilities for your actions and she never sugar coated anything, so I was used to her giving it to me raw and uncut. Not only that, but she didn't believe in abortions. Well, she did, but only in drastic instances like rape or some other extreme situation. So for me to be standing there even pretending like I was going to get one had her pissed and this I was sure of.

"You don't understand, Tasha. This is not how it's supposed to be," I cried, feeling like shit for even contemplating getting rid of a child that I only knew existed for a few moments.

"I may not understand because I'm not in your situation, but I get it. You didn't plan this for yourself and that's okay. Things change. I'm not saying that it will be perfect, but shit, you're grown, Kennedi. You're twenty-three and you take care of your damn self. You have your own house, your own car, and your running a successful business by yourself," she explained. "So what if things aren't right on track. You can make the shit work. You're pregnant with a child that didn't ask to be here, so you have to do right by it."

Hearing Tasha's speech really made me feel like crap because she was right. Here I was about to break down and have an anxiety attack, and it wasn't even the end of the world. There are lots of women who have children way younger than me, and they make it with less. I am an adult, with my own money and I'm capable of doing this. Thoughts of Ethan immediately cloud my mind. *What is he going to say? How is he going to feel? Will he want to be involved in his child's life? Will he claim the baby isn't his?* All kinds of questions jump out at me at once. So many that I instantly got a headache. Walking back over to my bed, I took a seat and placed my head into my hands. I felt the weight of Tasha's body beside me before her hand gently started to rub my back.

"It's going to be okay, Pookie," she told me. "If you don't have anybody else you know I'm here, and that's until the very end. If Ethan doesn't want to step up, it'll be *our* baby." Even though I laugh I know that she's dead ass serious.

"I know. Thank you, Tasha, for always being here when I need you most," I responded lying my head on her shoulder.

"Of course. You know your bestie has your back."

"And I have yours."

An hour later, as Tasha laid sleep in my guest bedroom, I sat on my bed staring aimlessly into at the ceiling. Tears rolled down my face and dropped onto my pillow. The television was playing, but I wasn't watching it all. I couldn't concentrate even if I wanted to. My mind was on other things. Climbing out of the bed, I grabbed some clean clothes, walked into my bathroom and turned on the shower. Once I got the temperature to what I wanted it to be I undressed and stood in front of the vanity mirror. With red and puffy eyes, I just stared at myself for a moment. I looked a mess. Even after the talk with Tasha I was still all over the place. I had made up my mind to keep the baby but my emotions were still on edge. I'd been crying for the last hour nonstop, but I'd decided that I was going to quit right now. There would be no more tears. I'm going to pull up my big girl panties and deal with this head on.

After removing the scrunchie from my wrist, I brushed my hair back into a semi-neat ponytail and secured on top of my head before putting on my plastic shower cap. Running my hands down my body, I place them on my flat stomach. Although I couldn't be anymore than a few weeks, I knew that there was a growing life inside of me. Moving from side to side, I poked out my belly and tried to imagine how I would look once I started to pick up weight. Realizing that I must look ridiculous I laughed and make my way into the shower to wash up. As the water ran down my body, I allowed it to also wash away all the doubt and anxiety that I was feeling at the moment.

Twenty minutes later, I'm out of the shower, and feeling like a new woman. Once I lotioned up my body, I got dressed and climbed into the bed. Picking up my phone, I remember that I never responded to Ethan's text message that he'd sent me earlier. After glancing at the clock and seeing that it's a little past eleven, I started to wait until tomorrow to send him the message, but something told me that he just might be up. Going to the messaging app, I tap on his name and pause. I'm not even sure what to type. Don't know if I should respond to Ethan's earlier message or let him know that I'm pregnant. After a few minutes go by I decide to wait until I see a doctor to completely confirm my pregnancy before I mention it to him. Now that I don't have to worry about breaking that news to him, texting seems too easy. I quickly type out a message and hit send.

ME: *Hey handsome. Sorry but I'm just seeing your text. I was busy with Tasha all day. Are you still up?*

Ten minutes go by, and just when I think that he's not going to respond my phone alerts me of a message.

ETHAN: *Yes, I'm just getting out of the shower. I've been thinking about you all day. I'm missing you something crazy.*

I can't help but smile at his message. It's something about
that man; he always knows exactly what to say to make me feel good. I'm in the process of typing him out a reply, when my phone rang in my hand. It's Ethan.

"Hello," I answered propping my pillows up behind me.

"Hey baby."

"Hey," I smiled.

"I didn't feel like texting. Can you talk?" he asked.

"Yeah, I can. What's up?"

"Nothing. I just wanted to hear your voice. I haven't talked to you since yesterday, and I missed you."

"I've missed you too," I replied meaning it. "I can't wait to see you again."

"Trust me, the feeling is mutual. I'm making some moves to make sure that we can see each other sooner rather than later," Ethan paused. "As a matter of face, how about I fly you out here for a few days?"

"You don't have to do that, I can fly myself out," I told him.

"Kennedi, how many—"

"I already know what you're going to say, and I'm sorry." I cleared my throat. "Let me check my schedule and see what I can do, and I'll let you know. I'm sure I can pull it off."

"Good, because I'm going through withdrawals and I need to be close to you."

"Boy hush," I giggled. "How are you going through withdrawals?"

"I just am. I can't lie, I got it bad for you," Ethan declared. "It's crazy because I've never felt this way before, and this shit is scary. You got me over here feeling like a sucka for thinking about you day in and day out." Hearing him say that made me feel better about our situation.

Although he didn't know anything about my pregnancy, at least I knew that he did care for me.

"You shouldn't feel like a sucka. I feel the same way about you too," I revealed.

"Well, I'm happy I'm not in this alone." There was a short pause on the line.

"Ethan?" I call out.

"Yeah, I'm here, baby. Imani's staying with me tonight and I heard her calling for me from her room. I'm going to call you in the morning. Is that alright?"

"That's fine. I'll talk to you tomorrow then," I said preparing to hang up.

"Will do. Oh… and Kennedi?"

"Yes?"

"I love you," Ethan expressed which shocked the hell out of me. While he's said it through text message before, he's never said it out loud. "Kennedi, are you still there?"

"Yes, I'm here."

"Did you hear me?"

"Yeah, and I love you too, Ethan," I replied.

"Goodnight."

"Goodnight."

After hanging up my phone, I continued to lay in my bed thinking. There are no more tears. Only thoughts of Ethan, me and our baby. Call me crazy, but somehow that conversation we just had let me know that everything was going to work out.

CHAPTER 21

Chace

If I ever needed God to get me out of a situation, now was the fucking time! First off, I was beyond embarrassed when my brother caught Jerome at my house. That day I could have shit bricks when Marquise called my phone and told me to tell Jerome to bring his ass outside. When I relayed the message to Jerome, that nigga was just as scared as I was. That right there was confirmation for me to leave his bitch ass alone. I know my brothers are savages, but a man still shouldn't let another man put fear in his heart. Seeing Jerome bitch up and start stuttering almost caused to me to laugh at his ass in his face. Instead, I told him to hurry up and get the fuck out of my shit. Shortly after I kicked his ass out, my brother came barging through my door and cursed my ass out!

"What the fuck you call yo 'self doing Chace?" *Marquise got in my face and snatched up my arm.*

I tried to snatch away from him, but he held a tight grip on me.

"It's not what you think, Quise." I called him by his nickname.

235

"Not what I think? Then tell me how the fuck that soft ass nigga Jerome ended up over here at your house while your husband not here?" Marquise asked as he released my arm, and shoved me lightly. I was stuck on what the fuck I was about to say to him. One thing my brother despised was a liar, and I was starting to become that to him. "And don't stand yo' ass there, trying to think of a fucking lie either. I already knew you were creeping with that nigga. Soon as your big mouth ass friend put that bug in my ear that night at the club, I started keeping a close eye on that nigga. I purposely gave his ass a pick-up close to here, just to see if he'll come this way, and he took the bait. Now, my question to you is, how the fuck can you go against the grain and fuck with one of my workers' when you know I don't allow that shit?" Marquise stared me dead in the face, waiting for me to answer him.

Right now, I felt like I was little girl again, and that he was chastising me for skipping school or some shit. Marquise has always been that strong headed, father figure and he didn't hesitant to whoop my ass back then like one either.

"Quise, look. I was just fucking around with Jerome for some get-back to Ethan. I found out that his ass is fucking around on me with this other bitch." I answered, trying to turn this situation around.

Of course, I was telling the half ass truth, but my brother didn't need to know all of that.

"Come on Chace, stop trying me for a sucka. I may not say shit to you, but I know way more than you think I do. Ethan been fucking around with other bitches, and you and Jerome have been messing with one another for a while." Marquise exposed.

"Oh, so you knew Ethan was messing around and didn't say shit to me!" I yelled out with anger.

"You need to lower your tone with me. Ethan is a man with money and status, did you think he was just going to stay dedicated to one pussy? Come on lil sis, I taught you better than that. Any man, even the broke ones, fall to the temptation of fucking with multiple women; that's just the way we were created. And to make shit clear, I never get involved in other people's business, you know that."

"Then why are you so mad right now? You just said it yourself that no man will stay dedicated to one woman, so me fucking with Jerome shouldn't be a problem." I folded my arms across my chest, waiting to hear his double-standard ass answer; because I knew it was coming.

"It's a problem because you fucking with my money. A nigga like Jerome love these hood, dirty ass bitches, that worship the ground he walks on. But a woman like you, that

is total opposite of all that, is one he'll fall for. Then, once his mind is in the clouds from thinking about you, that nigga will start to slip with what he really needs to be concerned about; money. Stop acting like you new to this Chace, when I been giving you the game since forever. I don't know what the fuck is going on with you and Ethan, but to be fuckin another man in his shit is straight up disrespectful. Get ya shit together." With that said, Marquise left out of my house that day, and I haven't heard from him since.

Jerome on the other hand, was blowing my phone up before I put his ass on the block list. The way he reacted when my brother busted us that day, turned me completely off. I didn't want to have shit else to do with his ass, and hopefully, he'll get the picture. Wanting to be completely done with Jerome, and anything that involved him, I drove myself to the abortion clinic, almost an hour outside of town, only to find out that it was too late for me to get one.

I was on the table, ready to get everything over with. The doctor did the ultra sound to see where was the fetus so that he could perform the procedure, and that's when he told me that I was too far along for him to do so. I even tried to bribe his ass by offering him more money on the side to handle this for me, but his Mexican ass still refused. I jumped off the table, threw my clothes back on, and hauled ass out of there.

Now here I was, pregnant, and not sure who the fuck the daddy is. I know that I could wait this thing out, and just pray the baby is Ethan's; but the rest of these months was going to be torture.

Standing naked in my bedroom, I was looking at my body in my floor length mirror. I turned to the side, and noticed a little pudge forming. With Imani, I carried small until I hit my eighth month, and I'm guessing it'll be the same for this one.

"Damn baby, your ass looking nice." I turned around to see Ethan staring at me.

I didn't even hear him come into the room. He woke up early this morning to drop Imani off to this new summer camp she was attending. Shit, he was gone for so long, I thought that he must have just went to work from there. Grabbing my robe off the foot of the bed, I put it on.

"Nah, take that shit back off" Ethan commanded as he came over to where I was.

I recognized that look in his eyes with the way he was looking at me; he wanted some pussy. With my hormones jumping all over the place, I was just about to give it to him too. Sliding the robe back off, Ethan came up from behind me, and began to lightly kiss me on the back of my neck. I shivered as his kisses trailed from my neck, down to my ass cheeks.

"Hmm" I let out a soft moan.

It's been a minute since I had some of my husband's chocolate, so I was about to enjoy this. Ethan stood back up, and turned me around to face him. Taking my right breast, he put it in his mouth. I almost lost it, because my breast was so tender! While going in between both of my breast with sucking on them, Ethan took his hand and stuck two fingers inside my pussy.

"I see somebody ready for daddy" he whispered in my ear.

I know that he was referring to how wet I was. Pulling down his sweat pants he had on, I pushed myself away from him, and laid spread eagle on the bed. Ethan finished undressing himself, and climbed on top on me. When he entered me, I felt like I was floating on air. Sex when you're pregnant is the next best thing next to drunk sex. Ethan was slowing going in and out of me, and I was rotating my hips underneath him. Not able to take it much longer, I flipped him over, placed my hands on his chest, and began to bounce my ass up and down on his dick.

Ethan loved it when I took control like this, and it showed with all the moaning he was doing. Flipping me back over, Ethan started drilling into my pussy. The harder he went, the more wet I became. I felt my juices sliding down the crack of my ass, as my legs were now on his shoulders. We continued to fuck, until we both exploded. By the time we were done, I had cum roughly three times and was tapped out!

Ethan was laying next to me, trying to catch his breath.

"Damn, that was good" he finally spoke.

"Yes, it was. What came over you?" I asked.

"What you mean?" he replied, still breathing heavy.

"It's just been a while since we went at one another like that. After Imani had her accident, you seemed distance."

"I know, I just was trying to get my head together. The thought of almost losing our daughter scared the shit out of me. I ain't gone lie though, when it first happened, I partly blamed you" Ethan admitted.

"Why?" I asked alarmed as I sat up on my elbows, and looked over at him.

"Because she was home with you when it happened. But, then I came to the realization, that accidents happen all the time when it comes to kids, whether the parents are around or not. I'm sorry for thinking that though Chace, because I know how much you love our daughter." Ethan apologized.

I just laid back down and looked up at the ceiling. I wasn't shocked that Ethan blamed me, but I was caught off guard with him admitting it. Everything in my life right now was so screwed up, and it was about to get worse with this pregnancy. Now that I was too far along to get an abortion, I had no choice but to let Ethan know that I was pregnant; but leaving out the part where I wasn't too sure if he was the father.

"You okay?" I heard him ask me, breaking me from my thoughts.

"Yeah, I'm fine." I replied as I got up from the bed and headed into the bathroom to take a quick shower.

Once I stepped inside and the hot water began to beat down on my body, I suddenly had the urge to vomit. Not wanting Ethan to hear me throwing up, I just let loose in the shower instead of the toilet. I tried to be quiet as I could, while I was throwing up this nasty ass bile. Soon as I was done, I finished showering, and jumped out to brush and gargle.

Coming out of the bathroom, I found Ethan sitting on the edge of the bed with his back facing me. Walking around to where he was sitting, I stopped when I saw my phone in his hand.

"Ethan what the fuck are you doing with my phone?" I questioned as I went over and tried to grab it out of his hand.

Ethan stood up, towering over me, and held the phone from my reach.

"I needed to google an address really quick, and since my phone is downstairs, I decided to use yours. I go to your internet, and as I began to put in the address in your search bar, your history comes up. You want tell me why the fuck you were looking for an abortion clinic Chace?"

CHAPTER 22

Kennedi

The sound of my phone ringing caused me to rush out of the bathroom to see who it was. Just as I made it over to the nightstand to picked it up, the ringing stopped. After unplugging it from the charger, I saw that I had four missed calls and all of them were from Tasha. Adjusting my robe around my body, I took a seat on the edge of the bed, and tap her name. The line rings a few times before she finally answers.

"Hey boo," I spoke out of breath.

"Don't *hey boo* me, hoe. I've been calling yo' ass for the last few hours!" she yelled.

I giggled. "I'm sorry, boo. I took a nap when I got to my room, and when you just called I was finishing up in the shower."

"Humph, look at yo' ass. Couldn't wait to get the penis," Tasha laughed.

"I wish. I haven't even seen Ethan yet. He had some business to handle so I came back to the hotel alone. I'm going to meet him later in his skybox to watch the basketball game."

Since Ethan was unavailable, I headed to the hotel straight from the airport. When the driver dropped me off, I went up to my room to unpack my things. With me staying here in New York for the next week I refused to live out of my suitcase. I had originally planned to go out to get something to eat, but before I knew it I was knocked out in the bed. I don't even remember being sleepy, but apparently I was. Once I woke up from my nap, I took a shower and that's where I was coming from doing when Tasha called.

"Oh damn, and here I was calling you all out your name. I was calling to see if you'd made it safely, you know, since you never texted me like you said you would."

"Yes the hell I did," I told her. "I texted you on the car ride here. Hold on." I pulled the phone away from my ear and went to my messaging app. "Girl, the text is still typed out on the screen. My slow ass forgot to hit send."

"You damn nut. Had me worried and shit. I thought Ethan's ex-bitch had found you and cut you up in little pieces," Tasha cracked.

"Yeah fucking right. That hoe ain't crazy."

"You ain't lying. Anyway, have you thought about how you're going to tell him your news yet?"

"I did, but I'm nervous as hell," I told her.

It had been two weeks since I'd taken the pregnancy test and found out I was expecting and one week since it was confirmed by my doctor. Since then I'd been trying to figure out how I was going to break the news to Ethan. I knew that I was coming up to New York to visit him, so I thought that it would be best to tell him face to face, that way I could read his expression and see what he really felt about it. People can tell you anything over the phone, but their up close and person reactions can't be faked.

"OK, don't keep me waiting, bitch. Share the fucking details," Tasha urged.

"Yo' impatient ass!" I yelled laughing at her anxious ass. "Well, I got this small gift bag from Walmart, and inside will be this cute little onesie that I ordered from Etsy that says, Hi Daddy, I can't wait to meet you."

"Awww, that's cute."

"I know right?" I agreed. "I also put the pregnancy test in there, as well as one of the ultrasounds that I got from the doctor last week. You can't really see anything but a tiny little sac, but he'll get the point."

"I'm all excited and shit like I'm the daddy," Tasha laughed. "I should've came with you."

"I wish you could have, because I'm a nervous wreck right now. I'm eager to get it over with, but I'm also afraid because don't know how he's going to react."

"Don't stress about it too much. I hope he takes it well, but you already know how I feel. Whether he steps up or not, my niece or nephew will be good."

"I know, it's just that… although I know that everything will work out, I do want him to be in his child's life," I sighed while getting up from the bed. I made my way over to the desk, grabbed a few pieces of tissue out of the box and dabbed at my now misty eyes. I know I said I wasn't going to cry anymore, but when it came to this situation, I couldn't help it.

"If he's as good of a guy as you say he is I really can't see him not wanting to do that," Tasha rationalized. "He has a daughter already and from what you tell me, he adores her."

I sniffed. "He does. Talks about her all the time."

"See, well you have nothing to worry about. Stop crying."

"How did you know I was crying?" I asked still wiping my tears.

"Because I'm your best friend and I know everything about you," Tasha said and I smiled. "Now get your naked ass dressed. The game starts in an hour and a half."

"I'm about to," I replied grabbing my oil off of the dresser. "I love you, bestie."

"I love you more. Don't forget to call me later and let me know how it went."

"Ok"

"I'm serious. No matter what the outcome is. I'm available to hop on a flight if you need me."

"I promise I'll let you know. I'll talk to you later," I said before we both disconnected our call.

With the oil in my hand, I take a seat on the bed and apply it evenly all over my body. With that out the way, I reach for the cream colored bodycon dress that I'm wearing, which is lying on the bottom of the bed and stand up. Since I'm not wearing any undergarments, I step into the dress and pull it up over my shoulders. It fits perfectly; not too tight and not too loose. Once I slip my feet into the matching thin strap sandals, I secure them around my ankle and make my way into the bathroom. There, I walk over to the mirror and finally remove the silk scarf from my head. My hair is still pin curls up from when I left the salon this morning to keep my curls in place, so all I have to do is remove the clips and I'm all set in that department.

With my toiletries bag in hand, I opened it up and removed the few items that I needed. Since I'm not a big fan of a bunch of makeup, I do it light. I apply a little eyeliner, mascara and lastly a coat of M.A.C Toupe lipstick, before topping it with a small amount of gloss. When I'm finished I take each of the clips out of my hair, and allow my curls to fall. After applying a little argon oil to my hands, I run my fingers through my hair until I'm satisfied with the results. Once I am, I go back into the bathroom to get my clutch and the bag that I planned to give Ethan. Butterflies are present in my belly. It's so bad that I immediately feel nauseous and my head starts to spin. Taking a seat on the bed, I closed my eyes and take a few deep breaths. It takes all of five minutes before I'm back calm again. Getting up from the bed, I grabbed my purse, the room key and bag, and headed out the door.

I make it to the lobby in no time, and once I step outside, the male driver is already waiting for me. After taking another deep breath, I step into the now opened back door and climb inside. Moments later he cranks the engine pulls away from the curb. As we drive, I sit back and think about what I'm about to do. While I'm excited about seeing Ethan again, the thought of being rejected is weighing heavily on my mind. To kill time, as well as calm myself down, I pull out my phone and fiddle with the apps. I soon up on Instagram, and just like any other day my direct messages are filled with people asking me all kinds of questions. They go from how much I charge to if I need a partner. Although I love my job, it can be annoying at time. My bio has contact information on it, which includes my email address, yet people continue to send me messages.

Twenty minutes later I feel the driver slow down, before the car completely stopped. Taking a look outside, I see that Madison Square Garden is lit up. There are so many people outside that you can barely see the sidewalk. Some are walking towards the building, while others are just standing around. Closing my phone, I placed it into my clutch and just sit there. Moments later the driver steps out, walks around the car and opened my door. As I step out the cool breeze hits my face. With my clutch and bag in hand, I thank the driver and make my way up the sidewalk to the front of the area.

My stomach is doing summersaults right now, but you would never know it by looking at me because on the outside I'm cool as a cucumber. As I strut up to the doors, all I can think about is the fact that in the next hour or so, I'll know whether Ethan and I are in this together or if I'm on my own.

Just thinking about it makes me want to turn around, run back to the car and tell him to take me to my hotel. I know I can't though, and because of that I trudge on. It's time to face the music, and even if the tune isn't one that I like, it's something that I have to deal with.

CHAPTER 23

Chace

My adrenaline was pumping as I was drove well over the speed limit. I had on a Nike track suite with a pair of Air Maxes to match, because I was about to fuck these muthafuckas up! A few weeks back when I was talking to Tricia, she suggested that I put this app on Ethan's phone that she used on her main nigga from time to time to see who his ass was texting. I was looking over his shoulder one day while he put in the unlock code on his phone, and memorized it. Ever since I confronted him the first time about Kennedi, the bastard put a lock code on his phone.

When Ethan was asleep later that evening, that was when I snuck into his phone and installed the app. Since then, it took everything in me not to bust him on his shit with the conversations I would see between him and that Kennedi hoe. Not only was I upset, but deep down, I was also hurt. From what I gathered, unless he was a good ass actor, Ethan loved this chick. He would tell her things that he has never even said to me!

I have never in my life since being with Ethan, have I ever felt threatened by another bitch he was dealing with; until now. Reading my husband profess his love to another woman did something to me on the inside; especially since I was pregnant. After Ethan discovered that I was pregnant, at first, he was pissed; mainly because he saw that I was looking for an abortion clinic on my phone's web browser. After I put on a show by crying and telling him that the only reason I was looking to terminate the pregnancy was because of how distant he was acting with me, he softened up.

By me turning it around on Ethan, and him already admitting to me earlier that day how he blamed me for what happened to Imani, he sympathized with me and told me that he understood where I was coming from, but that I wasn't about to abort his baby. Since that day, Ethan has been over joyed and excited about becoming a father again. It was crazy how he was now acting as this doting family man at home, but then telling this bitch how me loves and misses her.

I found out through Ethan's text messages to Kennedi that she was coming here to New York, and today she was meeting his ass at the basketball game, where he was attending with a potential client in the sky box. What really got me was not only did Ethan sneaky ass invited this bitch to come here, but he also was about to show her ass off to other folks as if he didn't have an entire family at home! Earlier today, Ethan mentioned to me how he was taking a client to the Knicks basketball game in hopes to convince him to sign with his company, but his ass conveniently left out the part of having his side bitch tagging alone.

I was on my way to the stadium now to confront Ethan and Kennedi together, and possibly whoop this bitch's ass if she got out of pocket with me. Our neighbor was watching Imani so she was good for now. Driving, I looked at time on my dashboard and saw that it was after eight p.m. The game had started thirty minutes ago so I'm sure Ethan and his bitch were settled into the sky box by now. The more I thought about it the faster I drove to get to the arena. After about another thirty minutes of driving, I was finally pulling up to the valet in the garage. Jumping out, I gave him my keys without grabbing a ticket. Going inside, I got on the elevator and pressed the button to the sky box. Looking up, my heart was beating so fast as I watched the elevator pass the floors.

I didn't know what I was about to walk in on, but I was prepared for anything. When the elevator stopped and opened, I took a deep breath as I stepped off. Looking ahead, I saw Anthony, the security guard who normally guards the sky box standing by the entrance. *Good,* I thought to myself as I approached him. Anthony knew me from all the times Ethan and I used to attend the games here. He was cool peoples, so I knew I wouldn't have a problem getting in now without a pass.

"What's up Anthony, how you been?" I said as I approached him.

By the look on his face, I could tell that he was shocked to see me. I knew it had something to do with the fact that he knew Ethan was already inside with another woman.

"Uh, Mrs. McKenzie, long time no see" Anthony stuttered.

"It has been a long time. Everything good with you?" I moved closer to the entrance to go inside.

"Uh… everything is good, are you going inside?" he continued to stutter.

"Yup, and before you try to stand there and make up some bogus ass excuse as to why I can't go inside, just know that I already know that my husband is in there with his side piece. So, since this is about to be family business, just move to the side and turn a blind eye." I reached in my purse, and pulled out two one-hundred dollar bills and handed it to them.

I knew the language Anthony spoke when it came to money, and just like I thought, he took the money from my hand and started walking down the hall away from the door. Taking another deep breath, I walked inside. The suite was nosey and packed with people watching the game. I stood there and looked around until I spotted Ethan. His back was facing me, but I recognized his frame anywhere. Walking over to where he was sitting, I stood on the side right of him as he was leaning over and whispering in to this woman's ear. Finally looking up, Ethan jumped up from his chair when he locked eyes with me.

"Oh shit, Chace what are you doing here?" he stammered.

Smiling, I walked around to the other side of where he was sitting and introduced myself to the guy that was sitting on the left of him.

"Hello, I didn't catch your name" I said to the gentleman.

"Hi, I'm David." He smiled as he took my hand into his.

"Nice to meet you, David. You must be the new client my husband is trying to sign. I'm Chace McKenzie" I said as I cut my eyes over at Kennedi.

The look on her face was priceless. She looked over at Ethan who was still standing there with this dumb as hell.

"Wife?" David repeated confused as he looked over at Ethan as well.

"Yes, wife. Oh, I'm sorry. You must have thought that Kennedi here" I pointed to her. "is Ethan's wife. Naw, she's just another one of his side chicks that he'll be bored with soon. Just like the other ones before her" I stated as I smiled at Kennedi.

"Ethan what the fuck is going on here?" Kennedi jumped up from her seat and got in his face.

"Hold up bitch." I made my way over to where her and Ethan were now standing. "The only woman that's gonna lay hands on this nigga here is me, his wife!" I flashed my ring in her face. "so I suggest you get the fuck up out of his face. Besides, don't act like you didn't know about me or had any idea that this man was taken!" I yelled.

By now, everyone in the sky box had turned their attention to us.

"I didn't! The only thing Ethan told me was about the mother of his daughter, and you guys weren't together anymore!" Kennedi screamed out.

Looking over at Ethan I wanted to punch him in his fucking face. This muthafucka straight played my ass by not telling this bitch that he at least had a wife at home.

"Yeah well, I am the mother or his child and his wife all wrapped up in one boo. Living together and sleep next to one another every night!" I emphasized.

Kennedi looked as if she was on the verge of crying. Looking at Ethan, she shook her head as he put his head down. Obviously realizing that Ethan wasn't going to say shit, Kennedi reached down and snatched up her things. The jerking movement caused the contents from this bag she was holding to fell out. I glanced down and my eyes quickly spotted something lying on the floor. Reaching down, I picked up what looked to be a onesie. As I read what it said on the front, I snatched it out of arms reach when Kennedi tried to take it from my hand.

"Oh really, so this is how it is, Ethan? You're about to have a baby by this bitch?"

I turned the onesie around with the words: *HI DADDY I CAN'T WAIT TO MEET YOU* displayed across the front of it.

"You should have brought two of these bitch," I turned to Kennedi. "because I'm pregnant as well."

To Be Continued...

CPSIA information can be obtained
at www.ICGtesting.com
Printed in the USA
LVOW03s1610090118
562393LV00002B/293/P